April Warnings

April Warnings

Stories

Mark Pleiss

velizbooks.com

Veliz Books' titles are available to the trade through our website and our primary distributor, Small Press Distribution (800) 869.7553. For personal orders, catalogs, or other information, write to info@velizbooks.com.

For further information write Veliz Books:
P.O. Box 920243, El Paso, TX 79902
velizbooks.com

ISBN: 978-1-9497-7603-4

Cover design: Minerva Laveaga Luna & Silvana Ayala

TABLE OF CONTENTS

For my Dad, who taught me what a snipe is . . .

Snipe Hunting

There's a story about a priest who got taken up by a twister not far from here. He and his congregation disappeared into the sky. About a week later they found him on the highway praying the rosary as he walked. A farmer recognized the priest and asked if he wanted a ride. As they headed to town the farmer asked what happened. A ceremony for the priest and the others was later that day. The priest nodded and said he didn't know where he'd been. His memory had been completely erased. People in town agreed that God had saved him, but the priest said it wasn't that. He said he was being punished. Some people think aliens abducted everyone in the church, but they let the priest go because he was a religious man. Most people think he was the only one in the church who made it out in time.

* * *

The pack of anvils forming out east begins to darken, and I notice our cattle moving to the ditch. They lie in a small huddle with their heads down, and their tails no longer sway from left to right, which means the bugs have gone away. Through the window, I yell to Dad, who's working on the west side of the house, to see if there's any weather approaching from that direction. It's common for one part of the sky to seem normal while a wall cloud sneaks in from the other. Over the years, people have developed a special sensibility toward the weather. They use the texture of the clouds, the feel of the air, and their animals' behavior to know when to take cover. My grandpa will still point to a puffy cloud in the middle of a sunny day and tell us it's going to rain. We'll laugh, but he'll just nod and spit out some more tobacco from under his lip. "Just you watch," he'll say again. Within an hour, we'll have to grab our things and head inside. Once I asked him how he knew what the weather was going to do, and he said he could just feel it. He said a lot of people used to have that ability, but not as many anymore.

The wind is picking up, and Dad tells me to make damn sure I haven't left anything out. There's a nasty one coming, and he doesn't want any surprises with the equipment. Inexpensive items assume unexpected identities during a tornado: putty knives become throwing darts, ball bearings become birdshot, screwdrivers become nails. Dad says we must be meticulous. Hacksaw frames, caulk guns, and bar clamps must be hung, strapped, and locked. Air compressors, power washers, and welding masks are placed in the truck, shut, and double-checked. I remember when a twister hit Sunnyside Trailer Park. It rained cats and dogs, barbecue grills, and oil filters. Our fields filled with sun lounges, bug tents, and used car batteries. The Gatsons lost their fat old tomcat, Biscuits, because they thought someone else had brought him in the house. A woman in Indie, a town several miles south of here, found him in a tree hissing at a spider.

Going into an underground shelter is a strange Midwestern ritual. We wait downstairs until Dad gives the signal. Then we move to the cellar in the back yard, enter the doors that lead beneath the earth, and pray the rosary until the storm passes. Dad sometimes turns on the radio, but it eventually goes quiet, and the Emergency Warning System fills the air. Finally, the sirens go off. Boys run to their mothers, and dogs tremble beneath the bed. Meteorologists and science teachers have been rehearsing the drills for years. Head to the basement. Stay away from windows. Cover your head with a blanket. If you're in a car, pull over and find a ditch. Never try to outrun a tornado. Storage items deemed unworthy of the garage inhabit every square foot of the shelter. There's a bag of Halloween costumes, empty spray paint cans, a riding lawn mower, and even a bag of human hair dad collected from the barber to scare away rabbits in the garden. Mom said her project last summer was to clean everything out, especially all the hair, but she quit after finding a brown recluse in an empty jar of Skippy.

I open one of the shelter doors and wait on the top step to view the clouds as they circle. Then I hear Grandpa's voice from the darkness a few steps below.

"It's a slow one," he says. "We got some time, but it'll hang around."

Dad runs inside the house and shuts the upstairs windows, bolts the back door, and quickly lowers the covers protecting the new kitchen window we installed last fall. It's my job to close the gate during a storm, and my mom looks nervous. I put my hand on her shoulder and tell her I'll be fine, but she uses her hand like a fly swatter.

"You stay right here. I'm not having my boy go to Oz for a few cattle."

"But Dad said . . . "

"Get in that shelter. Don't worry about your dad."

I count each of the seven steps on the way down. Then I move to the back corner, climb onto the riding lawn mower, and rest my head on my knees. As my body starts to relax, I feel someone shake my arm. It's Dad, and the wrinkles on his face look hard as leather.

"You know what the problem is, don't you?"

"Yes sir."

"I've told you a hundred times, haven't I?"

"Yes, sir."

"The minute this storm has a hiccup you're running out there and closing that gate. If the animals get out, you'll be spending the next month moving their carcasses from the side of the road."

"Yes, sir."

Dad shakes his head at me, but I ignore it. We've done this plenty of times. He'll mumble to himself and sit back down near Mom. Then they'll argue for a few minutes. He'll know she's right but won't admit it, and she'll let him have the last word. Once they've finished, he'll lower his head, and Mom will start her Hail Mary's. Before I know it, Dad will be asleep, and she'll be on her second decade.

Grandpa drags a 5-gallon bucket next to me and sits down. He looks at Mom and Dad over his shoulder, looks back at me, and then asks if I want to hear a story. Grandpa doesn't talk very often, but when he does, I like to listen. He fumbles with his words while his hands search for the protrusion in the breast pocket of his t-shirt. Grandpa always keeps his emotions in the three-inch tin of chewing tobacco near his heart. His fingers are shaky, but he gets his dip in. Storms affect him in strange ways. He stares blindly in all directions and starts to swallow his tobacco instead of spitting it on the floor.

He asks me if I'd believe a story he told me, even if it was a little crazy. He tells me it was something that happened a long time ago, before he really knew what to make of it. I tell him to continue, just as Dad gets the radio to work. The shelter fills with AM static, which changes in pitch and register as the dial moves at different kilohertz. I hope my favorite station will come on, but all I hear are the voices of weathermen. They're announcing funnels and floods, wind and rain, tornado watches becoming tornado warnings. This is the Emergency Warning System. This is not a test. Then there's a pause, and a woman with a Minnesota accent tells us to turn to 1110 for an important weather announcement.

Grandpa spits on the floor and rubs it in with his boot. Mom hates it that her father-in-law chews, but at least he doesn't smell like cigarettes. Grandpa tells me his dad was hard on him too, mostly because his mind wandered while he was working. Once he even forgot to put the tractor into park, and it damn near rolled into the creek.

He squeezes his bottom lip until it forms a fleshy U. Then he pulls on it and lets it go like a thick rubber band.

"There were still wagon tracks on the prairie then. Some places you can still see them, but they're mostly gone now. The railroad came into town sometime later, or sometime around then."

He says he doesn't remember things like before. He says his memory has almost vanished completely.

"The tribe soon left, and the Irish came in to work. The Irish and the Chinese. The trains don't come by anymore, but back then the tracks had a purpose, lots of jobs and lots of movement. The house shook when the trains would come by, all lights flashing and engines pumping, like something from another world blowing across the prairie."

Grandpa's eyes roll back as he searches for more words. It's clear he isn't struggling to see the past. He wants to reveal something.

"I still don't know if it was a train," he starts. "But for some reason, I know it wasn't. It had to be something else. One night I got up because I heard a noise coming from out past the barn, so I went to check it out. Once I was away from the house I saw flashes. As I got closer, the lights started taking more shape, and the noises got louder."

Grandpa stops talking and looks behind his shoulder. The others continue listening to the radio or praying the rosary. He looks back at me.

"You're going to think I'm crazy. I never told this to anyone, not even Grandma. I swear I saw a space ship. It was out by the cemetery. I saw the lights, I heard the noises, and I even saw someone"—he looks behind him and spits—"or something driving the damn thing.

"The problem is that my words fail me. I have the picture of what happened in my head, but when I explain it, it doesn't make any sense."

Grandpa spits more tobacco from his shaking lip. Half of it lands on his knee, and the rest lands on my foot. It's thick and black, like used coffee grinds spilled from a filter, and it stains my shoelaces. But he doesn't notice what he's done. His mind is somewhere else.

"The next thing I knew I woke up in the cemetery. Sometimes I wonder if it took me for a ride that night and erased my memory. Everything around here starts looking the same after a while, but since then, time seems like it's stood still. It's like nothing new ever happens."

More falls from Grandpa's mouth, and he cleans his lips with the wool of his sleeve. I don't know if the story is true, but it feels as real as the tobacco and spit between us.

"Maybe I'm crazy," he says. "But I hope there's more out there than cornfields and silos."

Maybe that's why strange stories are always floating around town. People still talk about the formations at the McMullen ranch about an hour from here. There's a guy Dad knows, Professor Anderson, who came from the college in town to look at them. He said the circles were done with perfect geometry, straight lines and a clean grid. Professor Anderson is a friend of Dad's, and a lot of farmers talk to him about chemical mixes, new technologies, and the sort of stuff farmers don't learn from their dads. He said he didn't know what the circles were, but he didn't think they were from outer space. There's probably a pretty normal explanation for it, but I like to think it was something else, maybe something from the sky.

Grandpa keeps talking as the storm starts to fade. I don't know how long we've been in the shelter, but Dad is walking up the seven steps to the surface. He stops on the third step and turns around.

"Everyone stay here," he says. "Except you. Go close the gate and count the animals. I want to know whether we're spending the rest of the day on the highway looking for cows."

Mom gives Dad a look, but he ignores it. She tells me to take something before I go. The beads are as big as cherries, and a small man with long hair is attached to the cross at his limbs. It's her favorite rosary, and it hangs in the living room as a decoration. I tell her I'll be all right, that it will only take a minute, and she smiles as I try to fit the whole thing into my pocket. Grandpa tells me to be careful. He says something feels funny. The air isn't right.

"Just hurry up."

One cow is a big investment, lots of time, money, and grass. After my third recount I realize there's one missing. Hopefully it's a mistake. I close the gate, and thunder sounds above me. The last cow might not have gotten out. It could be in the drainage ditch near the cemetery.

Dad buried his mother there thinking the only remains were those of his family, but he discovered a cheekbone several yards from the grave. He was digging out a tough piece of earth while repairing a sinkhole, and it came up like a potato in his shovel. Dad ignored it, but Grandpa called Professor Anderson. He said the cemetery is filled with the bodies of Irish and Chinese immigrants who came to farm the land and build the railroad. Grandpa told the story to my brother, who used it to scare me. My brother said a lot of people died near our property while they were laying the track. Apparently, the soil was more difficult near our land than the engineers had guessed. They had to use dynamite to break through the rock and sediment. At that time, the mixes were unbalanced and unpredictable, and the Chinese were the only ones who would touch it. A lot of people lost their lives without any closure, and that's why Grandpa said the ground was still haunted.

I squint my eyes as I approach the ditch, and I make out

a cow through the vertical dashes of freezing water. She's lying on the ground, comfortably protected between two bushes in the decline toward the creek bed. She moans as I get closer, but the animal doesn't move. I pat the cow on the head, remove my rosary, and put it around her head. I pat the same tender spot on the cow again, and then I head to lower ground.

I soon hear my name. I call back in the loudest voice I can make, but the words crack in my throat. The other voice is strong though. It is low and consistent, hardened from years of giving orders. He has a few feet of rope wrapped around his right shoulder, and his face is expressionless. He makes a large loop, puts me inside, and tightens it around my waist. He kneels and feels the roots. He pulls on them to test their strength and then ties a cinch knot around the thickest part. He yells directly into my ear, but I can barely make out the words. I look to his mouth.

"Pull," his lips are saying. "As hard as you can."

Our muscles clinch, and the knot tightens. Dad grabs me again by the neck and takes me to my knees. We lodge ourselves beneath one of the roots, and I hear the words "hold on" as every leaf, ant, and crab apple heads to the sky.

Soon the debris becomes larger. Branches move like twigs and pinecones shatter against the trees. Cardboard, scraps of wood, and wheels from someone's shattered farm equipment move along the game trails with the wind's elusive shifts. I wipe my face, open my eyes, and see Dad using his feet to dig a hole. I join him, pushing and pulling the heels of my boots to create a wall of earth that can protect us from the debris. He must know the work is futile, but it's the best we can do.

My mouth is dry, and the saliva tastes sticky and sweet from the blood and sap accumulating around my face. My arms are burning from holding onto the branch. The wind doesn't seem like it has lost any power. I have to keep my eyes closed to protect them, but I feel Dad's arm across my chest, which keeps me firmly planted across the root grinding into my back and the hard, stubby object that digs into my temple. I yell to Dad that I have to let go.

I need to rest my forearms for just a second, but he can't hear anything. The wind is too powerful.

The funnel looks like it was crafted on a throwing wheel. It slowly descends toward us, and it feels like it's going to tear the ears from my head and the skin from my bones. My body suddenly begins to levitate, but the rope catches me in the air. Soon I return to the surface, and I hear my ribs crack. I think I hear Dad tell me that we're going to make it, but I can't make out the words. I force my eyes shut and see a swirl of colors. Then everything goes black.

* * *

I sometimes wonder what happened when Grandpa saw that space ship. I wonder what the little green men looked like, if they played with his head and then dropped him back into the field. The more I try to remember what happened that afternoon when I went to close the gate, the more I think I understand what Grandpa was talking about. I try to describe the power of the wind, the sound it made when it struck our bodies, and the color of the tornado's tail, white as a mushroom after a warm rain. The words come out, but they seem fake, like I'm describing a scene from a movie. Whether I try to or not, I see the funnel when I close my eyes, and I feel the wind when my father turns a stubborn screw or uses a hammer to pound a nail into a piece of wood. The ricochet of a bullet, the engine of a crop duster, or even looking down from a tall building sends me back to that moment, when I hear my father's words, "We're going to make it."

* * *

When I open my eyes the tree trunk, the bridge, and the cow are all gone. We're beside the cemetery, and Dad is sitting next to me. He says I'm bleeding from the back of my head.

"Sit down and wait here. I'll get the truck."

My eyes wander to my grandmother's gravestone, which

has been pulled from the ground. I move to put it back in place, but I become dizzy. I feel my cracked ribs and once again lose my breath. I roll on the ground and try to suck in air, thinking of every fish I ever left on the shore to die. That's when I see a strange piece of metal sticking out of the dirt. It looks like a metal container of some sort. I put it in my pocket as Dad's truck pulls up beside me.

* * *

The object was rusty and charred black from an explosion or a flame. I didn't know what it was, but I noticed there was something inside. I couldn't open it with my hands, so I used a small hammer with a pointed nose to open it. Suddenly a piece of paper fell out. There was writing on it, but I didn't understand what it said. There were no letters, just a series of strange symbols. There were also several drawings I couldn't clearly make out. They were little circles and lines that looked like someone's geometry homework. I wondered if anyone else would know what it was, and what it was doing in the cemetery. Grandpa was reading the newspaper when I showed it to him. He asked me where I got it, and I told him I found it in the cemetery.

"That's about right," he whispered under his breath. "That's about the spot."

He took the metal container from my hands and examined it thoroughly. When he finished, he asked for the piece of paper and examined that as well. His eyes carefully moved up and down, as though he was trying to comprehend every inch of what he was seeing.

"It's from the ship," he said. "The burning is from entry, and the writing is their alien language. I've never been more sure of anything in my life. But you can't tell anyone. They won't know what to do with it. They'll just take it away."

* * *

It's a short ride to the hospital in Hooper. Dad drives the truck, my elbow hangs out the window, and Grandpa sits in the middle nursing a beer between his thighs. He doesn't say anything, but he nudges my ribs with his elbow every few minutes to make sure I don't fall asleep. The house survived, but little else did. We lost the barn, most of the cattle, and a tree fell on our harvester. When Grandpa finishes his beer, he chucks it out the window and adjusts himself for a nap. Once his head starts to tilt backward, Dad tells me to roll up the window. The truck is silent without the moving air. I don't turn on the radio because I can tell Dad wants to say something, but he seems reluctant to say it. The only sound in the truck is Grandpa's snoring, which doesn't go away until we arrive.

Dad fills out some paperwork, and the doctor comes out after a few minutes. He tells him the tests might take a while, and that he should go next door and grab something to eat. The doctor feels my bones and asks me questions. He said I got a concussion and some busted ribs. He tells me everything will heal in a few months, but no football in the meantime. I head to the bar down the street. A tree has fallen through the front window, and there is shattered glass covering the floor. Dad sits at the bar with a pile of beer cans in front of him. I take the nearest stool and tell him what the doctor told me. He puts his enormous hand on my left shoulder and then it moves to the back of my neck.

"You know Grandpa was hard on me, too. His first was his favorite, and nothing was going to change that. Then your uncle died, just a little bit before you were born. Grandpa was different after that, and then once Grandma died, he started being, well, how he is now."

Grandpa sometimes tells me stories about when Grandma was still alive. He talks about the road trips they used to take when they were younger and how she would fix her hair for high school dances. I sometimes wonder if Grandpa really was a different person, or if maybe it was Dad who changed after his brother died. I catch him looking at himself in a mirror hanging between a pair of liquor bottles.

"Hey Al," he says to the bartender. "Get the boy a beer. He's had a rough day."

"He old enough?"

"Does he look old enough?"

"He's your boy?"

The man puts a can of beer in front of me. Dad puts a five on the counter and tells him to keep it. I take a long drink, but I can hardly keep it down. Dad asks how it tastes, and I tell him it's okay.

"When I was a kid Grandpa used to take me snipe hunting," he says as he finishes his beer.

"What's a snipe?"

"It's a small, long-beaked bird that only comes out at night. You can always hear them on full moons, but sometimes they come out on other nights. They prefer the moonlight, and they also like to eat the bugs that come out after dusk. They have a funny mating call, and they make a small tapping noise with their feet. They're damn good eating, and you can catch them if you know what you're doing. You have to walk out into the cornfield and hide beneath the brush that gathers beneath the stalks. You bring a black garbage bag and tap on it. You want to make the snipe call–coo-coo-coo–every few minutes and then wait to hear if they call back. Once you call one in close, you have to set the bag up in front of it, get the thing to run in, and then close the bag as fast as you can. Grandpa would always tell me it was easy, but I never had much luck. One night he told me not to come home until I caught at least one."

"Did you stay out there all night?"

"Until at least two or three in the morning. He and his buddies were drinking and playing cards. When they finished, they came out and told me they had just seen one, but they didn't have a bag.

"The time your uncle took me snipe hunting was different. Grandma and Grandpa had already gone to bed, and your uncle took me to his favorite spot. He led me out into a cornfield way past where I had ever been. He said he'd be hunting just a few rows over, but he went back into the house and left me out there. After a few hours, I started calling for him, and then I started wandering through the rows. Everything looked the same, and my mind started playing tricks. I spent the entire night in the cornfield wandering and crying. When I ran out of tears I sat in the mud and fell asleep. Grandpa and the dogs found me in the morning. When he and Grandma discovered what had happened, they made your uncle detassel corn every day for a month."

I realize my sips haven't gotten me very far, so I take a long drink that gets me halfway through the can. Dad gets up from his stool and says that it's probably time to get home. I tell him I haven't finished my beer, and he tells me to bring it along. Grandpa wakes up when we open the door. He asks where his beer is, and I tell him he can finish mine. He takes a drink once we're on the highway, and then Dad takes it from him. He finishes the beer with a gulp, burps out the window, and tosses the can into the roadside ditch. The truck is quiet for a few minutes, and I catch Dad looking at himself again, this time in the rear-view mirror. I ask him if he's okay, and he tells me that he wanted to take me snipe hunting once, but he thought I'd never fall for it.

* * *

"It's a recipe for gunpowder," Professor Anderson told me. "It has the ingredients and the measurements. The lines and circles are directions for the scale." He asked me where I found it, and I hesitated before I told him. Then I showed him the container and told him it was inside.

"This of course is homemade," the professor continued. "Someone welded it together with pieces of scrap metal from the track. There was an oil drill that exploded on the property not far from here. Some old records say it was Indian land, but it might have been annexed by the county. I talked to some people in town, and they said a lot of people died, and the bodies were scattered for miles. They might be telling the truth, but you just

never know with the folks around here. They'll tell you anything if it makes a good story."

"But the symbols don't make any sense," I said. "It's like they're from another planet."

"I had a friend at the university take a look at it," Professor Anderson said. "It's not from another planet. It's from China. That's Chinese script."

* * *

Dad swerves a bit on the two-lane highway. At one point, he almost hits the guard rail, and Grandpa tells him to watch what the hell he's doing. I decide to turn on the radio and move the dial to my favorite station. Dad gets angry because he had it set how he wants it, and he reaches over to turn it back. I swipe his hand and tell him to leave it, which only makes him angrier, and Grandpa tells us both to knock it off.

None of us see it walk in front of us. It just appears out of nowhere, like it dropped right out of the sky. Dad hits the breaks, and I wait for blood to splatter on the windshield. But there's no broken glass, and there's no dead animal beneath our bumper. It's just standing there with its tail swaying from left to right. We get out of the truck and notice the animal is looking at us with a familiar gaze, and it has something around its neck that I immediately recognize. Dad has to use his entire hand to cover his mouth. Grandpa just spits on the road and rubs it in with his boot.

"The damn Martians," he says.

Final Rites

A farmer eventually found me on the side of the road, and he asked if I was a ghost. I told him I wasn't, but he seemed skeptical. Then he said he would give me a ride, and I said I'd take it if it wasn't too much trouble. He then asked if I was one of the priests from the church that went up in the storm. He said the service for me and everyone else was later that afternoon. I told him again I wasn't dead, but he still didn't believe me. I asked him if he had ever lost someone or something so great that nothing else seemed to matter, and surprisingly, he nodded. He said a long time ago he got sent to a war in a jungle, and everyone he met there got killed. He said he didn't know why he survived, but he confessed it couldn't have been God. I thanked him for sharing, but I told him my experience was different. He asked me where I wanted to go, and I gave him The Monsignor's address. He asked if he should take me somewhere else, like a hospital or a cemetery, but I told him I had business elsewhere. He asked me what my name was as I got out, but I just thanked him for the ride.

* * *

On the morning of the tornado I found The Monsignor in his favorite chair. It faced a window that looked out across two acorn trees and a forest that extended to Thompson Creek, and the Monsignor would spend his mornings there reading the catechism and observing the brown squirrels. In spring, the creatures would race across the yard and compete to fill their cheeks with seed and leftover bread. In the winter the animals grew scarce, but The Monsignor would still leave seed near the window, and a few of the animals would entertain him while he sat with a wool blanket covering his thighs. I knew the old man did not hear me knock, so I walked into the space directly behind his chair, stomped the ground with my left foot, and called his name. He must have felt the vibrations because he finally turned his head.

"Father Ellison you've startled me again," he said. "I do not understand why you refuse to knock."

I responded with the volume I always reserved for The Monsignor, which caused the squirrels to scatter.

"Perhaps I should just come through the back next time," I said. "Or perhaps you could get something for your..."

"I heard it again last night," he interrupted. "I had fallen asleep around 9 p.m., and I awoke as I often do, exactly one hour before sunrise. I reached for my book, but my mind was not ready for words, and so I closed my eyes and listened."

"What did you hear, Monsignor?"

"It was the owl again," he said. "It landed on my fencepost, and it angered the crows."

"How did you know it was an owl?"

"It was not just any owl. It was an Eastern Screech Owl. They are very small, and they make a very particular hoot, an eerie trill that is much different from the birds I remember from my childhood. During those years, a long-eared owl, the type you cannot find in North America, took up residence in the tree near our farmhouse outside of Dublin. My father, a man with a truly great love of animals, would have me sit beside him and listen to the bird call his friends in the night. It was a shrill, high-pitched noise that the neighbors would sometimes confuse for screaming children. But the long-eared owl in our yard was in fact a family man. His hen and the owlets survived through my adolescence, and it was not until after my summer at Trinity that he and the others went away. My father said they left only a few weeks after I did, which made both of our departures additionally arduous."

The Monsignor's eyes began to close, and I could tell he was back at his family home. I even noticed his neck as it slowly moved upward and to the right, like he was watching one of the birds spread its wings and search for field mice across the Irish countryside.

"My father was blind in his later years, but he still loved watching the animals. He had spent his life doing so, and he knew the exact moment of the day when the deer would move through the yard, and the foxes would peek into the rubbish. I will never forget when I returned home to see him before he passed, and he told me that a rafter of turkeys had been moving through our yard for the past few weeks. The news was surprising because of my father's condition, but also because such birds had disappeared from the island years before. Nevertheless, he described them in intimate detail. My father explained that there were four turkeys and that at least one of them was male. He said he could hear them as they approached, and he also said one of them had a bad foot. He claimed they would talk to one another as they looked for insects, snails, and spiders in the underbrush. He joked about shooting one for dinner, but my father never owned a gun. In fact, it was impossible to imagine him hurting an animal."

"So, do you believe there really were turkeys in the backyard?"

"I wanted to believe my father, but I knew there were no turkeys in Ireland. I imagined they appeared to him in his dreams, but I could never be certain."

The Monsignor repeated the words "I could never be certain"

under his breath while I prepared his breakfast. He ate one hardboiled egg on wheat toast with a single cup of coffee. Lately, however, I noticed that he only drank a few sips. I thought of omitting the drink from his breakfast entirely, but I feared that would offend him, so I continued to prepare the coffee and pour what remained down the sink when he finished.

"Have you heard it?" he asked me.

I ignored the question while I ran cold water over the single egg I had boiled on the stove.

"I know you can hear me . . . Have I ever told you my story? When I heard it?"

"Yes, Monsignor. In fact..."

"It happened while I was still in the seminary, on a hike while visiting Colorado. My grandmother died earlier that summer, and I had gone to her house in the mountains to help manage the estate. She had left her home in Cork after the death of our grandfather and purchased property in America. My grandmother knew many people who had gone there to work on the railroad, and she loved reading books about cowboys, Indians, and pioneers in the west. She especially adored the women who would hold together the homes while their husbands were hunting, playing, and dying in the foothills of the Rocky Mountains.

"Anyway, I was hiking her land with the two dogs she left behind, and I quickly became disoriented. The hours passed as I wandered unknowingly through the identical landscapes, aspens, and pine trees. Before I knew it, the sun began to creep below the mountains, and I became increasingly concerned about the animals around me. The woods were filled with moose, bears, and coyotes, but the mountain lions scared me the most. The black bears feared humans and would only attack if they felt threatened. The cats, however, were hunters and would gladly pursue human prey.

"It seemed like hours before the dogs found the path back to the house. I remember we approached the field surrounding the residence just as the sun began to disappear behind Long's

Peak. I was fortunate there was still light because I would not have seen the movement in the brush behind me. It had waited for the wind to change directions and for the dogs to get too far ahead to protect me. The signs posted at the park said to make yourself tall and yell if you were confronted by a bear, but not to do so for mountain lions. They only advised to fight back with anything you can. I yelled to the dogs, but I did not want to take my eyes away from the movement in the brush.

"I threw a small rock at the animal, but it only seemed to make the creature more focused. It soon revealed its eyes, those of a creature with a perfect predilection for hunting. I reached for anything I could use as a weapon, and my hands came across a large branch from a fallen pine tree. I called again to the dogs and then lifted the limb like a prehistoric man. It was seven or eight feet long, and it was heavy, the type of weight I could not have managed if my life was not in danger. The cat soon emerged from the weeds, and I could finally see its body. It was long, lean, and muscular, a stature made hard from long hunts, streaks of hunger, and nights of raw meat.

"The cat looked amused with me holding the branch. It licked its snout and then hurled itself at me. I was fortunate it took a bad angle, and I redirected the cat's thrust. However, I could not keep the weight of the branch in my hands, and it fell to the ground. The animal then got back to its feet and prepared to pounce again. Luckily the dogs had heard me, and they returned before it could attack.

"Maple and Olive were by no means the docile pets their names might suggest. They looked like huskies, but their eyes revealed the genes of wolves. One of them, I don't remember which, had a bullet lodged in its back. Grandma would let them out of their cages to follow their instincts during the day, and one afternoon she got a phone call from her neighbor, a rancher from miles down the road. He said the dogs had been watching his goats from atop the hill surrounding his property, and that day one of them took a calf by the throat and attempted to drown it in the river. He fired his rifle at a great distance, and the dog fell. When the man approached it, he was surprised to see the animal was still alive and that it was wearing a collar. Suddenly it sprang to life and ran back to my grandma's house where it would eventually recover.

"I was glad the dogs were as ferocious as they were, as they quickly got between the mountain lion and myself. One of them bit into the cat's hind quarters, and the other went for its belly. I ran to the house to fetch my grandmother's rifle, but when I returned the cat was gone, and Olive was licking a gash on Maple's chest. The claw had entered her rib and slid its way into the dog's organs. The blood was dark, and it covered my hands as I tried to suppress the wound. I knew my work was futile, but then I heard a voice, and it told me to clean my hands. I removed my long-sleeve flannel shirt and wiped the sticky liquid that had dried down my forearms.

"Then I heard the voice again. It told me to place my hands atop the dog's body, which was convulsing with pain and blood, and I said the words that were given to me. The blood soon began to clot, and the skin from the wound began to tighten. I took the dog in my arms and carried it to the river. I laid the body on a bed of weeds and continued to recite the words the voice told me to speak. After that, I cupped my hands with water from the current and poured it over the wound. The blood washed away, and I noticed that the gash had healed. First the dog's tail began to beat against the earth, and then its ears sprang upward. It licked my ear as if to thank me, and then both dogs disappeared into the woods. I waited for them to return that night, but they never did, as though they had been called to return to the wild."

I looked at The Monsignor with doubt, but he assured me every word was true.

"We should hurry up," I said. "Father Nguyen is surely waiting for us, and I still need to meet with the old woman."

* * *

We mostly rode in silence as we moved toward The Monsignor's address, but I could tell the farmer was thinking about something. I had my own thoughts to organize, but I decided to ask him what was on his mind.

"It's funny," he said. "I've never said anything about that jungle to anyone."

The man wore a cream-colored cowboy hat, blue jeans, and a denim jacket with scattered buttons and rhinestones. I asked him why he thought he shared what happened to him during the war, and he smiled and said he didn't know.

"Maybe because you're a priest," he said. "Or maybe because you're dead."

I asked him what he thought happened to his friends that died in the jungle, and he said the birds showed up first, and then everything on the jungle floor.

"We don't return to dust in the end. We're consumed by bugs and earthworms."

I told him that's not what I meant.

"You must mean their souls," he said. "Well, they aren't in heaven or hell. That doesn't happen to people who go like that. It happened too fast. They didn't have time to know or prepare. They probably don't even know they're dead. I'm guessing they're trying to figure out what happened or are still trying to find their way back home. It wouldn't surprise me if that jungle was full of them, and one of the roads led directly back to Baxter County."

* * *

The air was unseasonably warm for spring, and I noticed the sky was as pink as an advent candle.

"It looks severe," The Monsignor told me.

"Likely a tornado," I said.

"It is difficult to imagine the misfortune of being caught in a tornado," he replied. "Think about it, Father Ellison. What is the possibility that the atmosphere would engage in rare cyclical movements, stirred on by the mix of warm and cool air in the atmosphere, and do so in the very space and time that a person occupies? I simply cannot believe such an event would be a product of circumstance. I could only say that it would be part of our Father's will."

I nodded and continued to walk toward the church.

We arrived fifteen minutes before mass, and the altar boy was already dressed. He had lit the candles in the sanctuary, set out the chalice, wine, and water to be blessed, and removed the precious jewelry from the safe. The altar boy also had hung The Monsignor's white rochet on the mirror and placed his red chasuble on a hanger beside the wine cabinet. The Monsignor retrieved his Bible from the counter and an ornamental ring he only wore during mass. He placed the adornment on his finger and then thumbed through the pages for the first blessing. It is tradition for the priest to select the first reading for the altar boy, who opens the book and holds it while the priest reads to the congregation. Unfortunately, The Monsignor's book was becoming unmanageable.

The altar boys could no longer find the daily readings because the bookmark had become lost in a confusing assortment of pastel-colored ribbons that only The Monsignor knew how to interpret. Furthermore, The Good Book had almost doubled in size to account for the cataracts of its reader, and its weight continued to grow with the weekly addition of prayer cards from funerals, weddings, and baptisms. The altar boys joked that holding the book was like cradling a baby elephant, and my heart sank for the many young men who couldn't support its weight. The thud of the Bible would echo across the pews and spook the pigeons in the bell tower. Sometimes the altar boys would gather their strength and try again, but other times they would hold back tears as they collected the prayer cards from the floor—all while The Monsignor recited the rest of the prayer from memory.

* * *

"Have you seen someone die?" he asked.

I told him it was part of the job. You show up when men and women are likely to pass, and you say a special blessing, absolve their sins, and offer last communion.

"It's called The Anointing of the Sick," I said.

"What happens if you don't get to them before they pass?" he asked.

"Only God knows the answer," I said. "But there's a lot of theories."

"Are any of them true?"

"I'm not sure, but I'll never forget the first time I administered a final blessing. I had just moved to Baxter County, and I received a call from a terrified nurse who said a man at the hospital was screaming at the top of his lungs for a priest. I drove over and found him chained to the hospital bed. He began to calm as we spoke, and he admitted that he used to worship the devil. He seemed relieved that I would still perform the blessing, but things felt strange as we proceeded. The air became cold as we spoke, and the lights flickered in the room as he confessed his sins. He blasphemed in three languages when I finished, and he hissed like a snake before he received communion. The lights went out in the room after the man passed, and the air turned so cold I could see my breath. That night I saw the man again in my dreams. He had no arms, his skin was covered with scales, and he had a tail extending from his coccyx. However, he had a smile on his face and seemed to be thanking me, like I had saved him before he lost the final piece of his soul."

* * *

Father Nguyen stood to greet us and then sat back at the wood table in the back of the sacristy. His black hair matched his outfit, and he used a pair of wire-framed glasses and the light from a stained-glass window to read from his prayer book. In the center of the glass was an image of The Virgin holding a sheep, and on bright days the sun would cast the blue of Mary's gown across the scripture. Today, the growing clouds brought little light upon Father Nguyen's pages and instead projected a dark shadow over the man and his book. For many, the arrival of the priest signaled the uncertain future of the profession. The lack of young men was being felt in many small towns, and those of Baxter County were no exception. The crop of candidates from local farms had diminished, and the bishops had to look abroad to fill their diocese with energetic faces capable of carrying the mission forward.

Unfortunately, many of the priests from abroad spoke with accents that were difficult to understand. The tone and register of their "r's" and "o's" often missed the mark, and dramatic words during culminating portions of the mass would come out wobbly or disproportionately melodramatic. Father Nguyen's attention to the pronunciation of "Christ" was particularly problematic. He said the word with three syllables instead of one, and he often fumbled the vowels in "blood," which made him sound like a vampire while performing the act of transubstantiation.

The language was only one of Father Nguyen's challenges. The parishioners of St. Michael's had been dwindling for decades, and they were mostly comprised of older couples with men who had returned from wars in Japan, Korea, and Vietnam. They said they could not understand what the Chinese priest was saying, and some said he should go somewhere else.

The Monsignor put me in charge of dealing with the matter. I scheduled The Monsignor and myself for the early masses and assigned Father Nguyen to the afternoons. These later services were mostly populated with young families who were more concerned about their kids than the national origins of the officiants. They brought their children every Sunday and raised them Catholic, but the little ones would eventually grow up, stop attending mass, and leave Baxter County.

I left The Monsignor in Father Nguyen's care and headed toward the house of the old woman who required final rites. I proceeded by foot on the shoulder of the highway and moved quickly past wheat and corn fields, cows, and hay barrels. A few cars passed me, and the drivers lifted their index fingers when they saw my collar. I watched the darkening sky and flashes of lightning in the distance, but I soon became distracted by a large truck heading toward me. It was carrying a blade from a wind turbine, and its force almost knocked me to the ground. It was like seeing a white whale blow across the prairie, which made me think about the ocean and everything else outside Baxter County.

The old woman had been blind her entire life, and she lived with an unusually intelligent golden retriever named Scarlet. The door behind the screen was open, but I still knocked before I entered. Scarlet met me at the door and gestured for me to follow. The dog led me to a dark room where I found the woman in bed. She was small, frail, and cold. She confessed her sins, received her anointment, and then received communion directly on her tongue. When we finished, she asked if I would pray with her, which I did, and then I asked if she would like me to say an additional prayer for her soul.

Her fingers trembled lightly in my palms, and she cried during the blessing. When we finished she said she was thirsty and asked the dog to get her a glass of water. I told her I could do it, but she insisted it was Scarlet's job. We began talking about life, sickness, and death, when suddenly I heard a rumbling in the kitchen. It was the sound from an electric ice crusher on a refrigerator door. It seemed to be coming from the kitchen, and it was followed by a tight stream of water that crackled as it hit the ice at the bottom of the glass. The woman asked me to continue reading, which I did, but I had to pause again when Scarlet returned to the bedroom. His head was cocked to the right, and he held a glass of ice water in his mouth. The woman took the glass from the dog, and I helped her take a sip and then place it on her nightstand. She then told Scarlet that she was hungry.

I continued reading, but the woman interrupted. She said she was surprised that a man like myself had dedicated his life to God and asked why I became a priest. It was a question I had been asked by family, friends, and parishioners for years, but I wondered what she meant by "a man like myself." I wondered if she thought I did not look or talk like a priest, or perhaps the blessing was not performed as it should have been. I wondered if she thought I was an imposter, and then my mind drifted to the mountain lion in Colorado, the humiliation of the altar boys when the baby elephant slipped from their hands, and whatever phonetic rule guides the pronunciation of the two vowels in blood.

"It was my calling," I said, and she nodded as though I had given her the right answer. I then asked if I could ask her a question, and she said I could.

"What is it like to be blind?"

She smiled at the question and told me to close my eyes. After a few seconds everything went black, and I asked her if that was what it felt like. She laughed and said no, at least not for her. She said to imagine the space exactly two inches behind my head.

"It's like that," she said.

I kept my eyes closed while I tried to comprehend her meaning. Then I decided to be forthcoming.

"Can I ask you another question?" I asked.

"Of course," she said again.

"What did you mean when you said, 'a man like you?'"

She seemed confused.

"You said, 'why would a man like you have dedicated his life to God?'"

"Oh," she chuckled. "It's just that you are a very attractive man."

Her comment made me think of The Monsignor and the eerie trill of the Eastern Screech Owl, and then the tornado sirens sounded across Baxter County. The horn turned three hundred-and-sixty degrees, and the volume gradually increased as it moved in our direction. The old woman closed her eyes during the brief period that the warning was at its loudest. I thought for a moment she had fallen asleep, but I touched her hand and realized she had passed. A chilly breeze swirled around my shoulders as the siren decreased in volume, and then the air rocked the door as it disappeared into the kitchen. I felt the woman's wrist again, and her body had gone as cold as the gush of air that had circled me. The muscles in her face had relaxed, and I said a final prayer for her safe passage to the other side.

I wiped my face clean of the emotions that had followed the woman's departure and then realized I had to get back to The Monsignor. I told the woman I would send someone for her, but I had to find safety first. I exited through the kitchen and saw Scarlet lying on the floor eating a sandwich. On the counter there were two open bags of lunch meat, a can of mayonnaise, and a jar of pickles that hadn't been opened. I told the dog I would be back, but it cocked its head like it didn't understand what I was saying. I told it again I would be back as soon as I could, but it just returned to eating the sandwich.

*　*　*

"In the Christian tradition," I told him, "the souls of the dead go to heaven, hell, or purgatory. The first is the ultimate reward for a life dedicated to Jesus Christ, but the second is more important. Without it, immorality goes unpunished. Purgatory, however, is less clear. It isn't up or down, and it isn't punishment or reward. Some say it's populated with babies who were never baptized, but others say that it's limbo, which is something entirely different. Others say purgatory is the place where souls wait until they receive enough prayers from those on earth to erase their sins. One priest said a single prayer erases a single sin, but others say the math isn't that tidy. Others have a different theory. They say purgatory exists on earth, in places the deceased spent their lives or ended them. They say many might not even know they're dead; they're just roaming the earth until the number of prayers aligns with the number of affronts committed. It's hard to say if any of it is true, but it's hard not to think about sometimes, especially when you're wandering the highway. You hope someone picks

you up, but you don't know where they're going to take you. They could give you a lift home or they could take you somewhere very different."

* * *

A wall cloud was hovering over the church when I returned. It looked like something from the Bible, a wrathful and apocalyptic force sent to eliminate our sins. The Monsignor was offering his final thoughts to the parishioners when I arrived, but only a few deaf elders were listening. The mothers and fathers of the younger families were gathering their baby bags and taking their children down the aisles. Others were warning everyone not to leave because it was already too late. Father Nguyen rushed through the doors behind me. He said he was trying to open the tornado shelter, but the key wasn't turning, and the winds had just taken the swing set behind the church.

"We have to get below ground," he said.

The Monsignor, who always preached with his eyes closed, remained oblivious to the events taking place around him. He spoke of Genesis, the creation of the animals, and God's day of rest, but it seemed like he was predicting the apocalypse. I told Father Nguyen to let me try the key, but I hesitated when a tree branch moved like a torpedo through the stained-glass window behind the tabernacle. The log landed only a few feet from The Monsignor, who finally opened his eyes. I told everyone to cover their heads and move away from the hanging candelabra that had already welcomed the six weeks of Lent.

I told Father Nguyen to stay with the parishioners, and I would run outside, unlock the shelter door, and then give the signal. He told me it was too dangerous, and that he should go instead. I shook my head and lied, saying the lock was sticky and required a trick The Monsignor had taught me years ago. The candelabra then fell from the ceiling and shattered in the middle of the church. The nails in the roof began to fall to the floor, and we could hear the frame of the ceiling begin to creak and bend. I told Father Nguyen to keep everyone calm until I returned. He said he would do his best, and then I ran out the door.

I could feel something from St. John and the Book of Revelation directly above me. I fell to the ground when I arrived at the shelter door, and I lied as low as possible while I tried to turn the key. The lock was more petulant than usual, and I was forced to pause when a gust of wind grabbed me by the legs. I let go of the lock and grabbed the iron bars that opened the doors that led into the earth. I held on tightly while my lower half was being pulled into the sky. Larger pieces of wood, metal, and plastic cut across my arms and face, and I soon realized that my toes were pointed upward. My arms burned, but I kept my grip until the winds changed direction, and my legs then fell the length of my body and slammed into the ground. Pain surged from somewhere near my feet, but I ignored it, and I focused on the lock.

The mechanism finally released, and I opened the doors. I pulled my body into the stairwell and used my arms to get down far enough where I was safe from the winds. I thought both my shins were broken, so I did not try to stand and instead looked for something that I could use to signal Father Nguyen. The light from the open door illuminated a slightly discolored American flag that The Monsignor had hung while many of the parishioners were in Vietnam, and I used my arms to pull my body toward it. I grabbed the pole, stuck it down the back of my shirt, and then army crawled back up the six or seven stairs that returned me to the surface. Once at the top, I removed the flag and began to wave it toward the church in the hopes that father Nguyen would get the message.

Unfortunately, I could not hold the weight of the flag, and I blacked out momentarily from the pain in my legs. When I came to, Father Nguyen was dragging me into the shelter. He opened a box of props from the nativity scene in storage, and he used the stuffing from baby Jesus' manger to make me a soft place where I could lie. Then he fashioned a tourniquet from Joseph's tattered rags and used two plastic donkeys to elevate my injured legs. He finally went up the stairs to signal the others, but he suddenly slammed the door shut and returned to the bottom of the shelter.

"The tornado is right above us," he told me. "It'll take me and everyone else, just like the swing set."

I asked him if the church was still standing, and he told me it was.

"God will protect them," he said. "And if he doesn't, he'll take them to heaven."

"Or to Oz," I said with a smile.

The tornado sounded like the semi-truck with the white whale. I didn't know what to say to Father Nguyen, but I felt like he needed some peace, so I asked him what he was feeling.

He didn't respond and instead asked me if he had ever told me about his calling.

"No," I replied.

"Good," he said. "Because it was all a lie."

I opened my mouth to speak, but we remained in silence until Father Nguyen walked up the stairs and opened the cellar doors.

"I can't just sit here," he said.

I knocked aside the donkeys and dragged my body up each step behind him, pleading for him not to go. I eventually got my top half out of the shelter, but I did not see Father Nguyen. I could only see the parishioners at the window. They were waiting for a miracle, but it was already too late. They could not see the funnel as it slid from the wall cloud directly behind them. The tornado doubled in size, and then it doubled again. In an instant, the twister had become four or five times larger than the church, and it was clear that everyone was doomed. The roof did not blow off until the twister was ten or twenty yards from the building, and the foundation stayed connected to the earth until the final moments. The church made the sound a popcorn seed makes when it goes up a vacuum cleaner, and everything I had worked for was gone.

I put my face into the cold mud in front of me, and that was when I heard the voice.

* * *

Some say they found me dead in the shelter, but I remember getting up at some point. I mostly roamed the highways, not in any real direction, before I got a ride from the farmer, and he dropped me off where I wanted to go. I knocked before I entered, and I stomped the floor a few times as I approached the chair. I walked to the window and looked for squirrels, but they were gone, and I soon saw myself in the reflection. I looked older than usual, and I imagined telling a skeptical younger man about the day I heard the voice. The silence was suddenly interrupted, however, by a noise in the bedroom. It sounded like someone was going through The Monsignor's things, and I imagined it was a family member or someone from the parish. I called out to let them know I was in the living room, but I did not get a response.

I decided to go to the bedroom and see who it was, but there was nobody there. I looked under the bed, just to make sure, and then I heard a noise in the kitchen that sounded like someone had gotten out a pan. I followed the noise, and again there was nobody there. Then the backyard door opened. The sound was clear as anything I had ever heard, and the door was in fact open when I approached, but there was nobody to be found. I walked through the door and sat on the steps that led to the grass. I peered into the trees to see if someone was moving through the bushes, but there was nobody there.

I went outside, and that's when I saw them. It was the old woman and The Monsignor, and they were watching a family of long-eared owls perched on the old man's fence post. I sat beside them and said I was glad they were alive, but neither responded. Then I told them that I finally heard the voice. I said it happened only seconds after the church disappeared. Still, neither of them reacted, and so I put my hand on The Monsignor's shoulder. He and the old woman disappeared when I did so, and then I was alone with the birds. After a while I heard a dog bark and thought it might be Scarlet, and the trill of another bird, maybe an Eastern

Screech owl, echoed from somewhere near Thompson Creek. The two younger birds shook their feathers and flew toward the noise in the trees, but the largest one, which I think was the oldest, remained. We stared at one another for a few seconds, and then it flew into the forest, and I started walking to my funeral.

The Worm Child

I knew a guy named Milliken, and he had a son we used to call the worm child. Each spring, rainwater filled the gullies and creeks of Thompson Creek, and it would wash earthworms from the soil. Flushed from the ground, the tiny creatures would writhe helplessly on the concrete, and most became the victims of shoes, fishermen, and robins. The worm child, whose real name was Robert, would always assist the creatures on his way to school. Sometimes there were only ten or twelve, but other times there were hundreds. God-fearing neighbors said the kid made them think about the parable of the starfish. In it, a man approaches a young boy who is throwing the creatures into the ocean after low tide. The man tells the boy he can't save all the starfish, and the child says that may be true, but he can always save this one. Robert, however, was not a prophet. He was just a kid who wanted to save the worms, and if it had been up to him, he would have spent the entire day on his knees moving across the sidewalk.

* * *

Milliken was different after Robert disappeared. He started showing up here on weekdays before noon. He also quit talking, and he would just stare at himself in the empty glass bottles lining the bar. Sometimes Milliken cocked his head to the left like a parakeet, and other times he'd mumble to himself and make hand gestures like a crazy person. He would also bring in books from the library and talk to people from the Sunny Side trailer park. Many thought they were part of a cult, and they'd go on about space ships and asteroids in the same way farmers would argue about pesticides and cattle. They talked about the Midwest like it was another world, like it was a distant planet or a universe far away.

Milliken came by not long before the tornado moved down Cedar Street. I met him at the entrance and said we were closed, but he didn't seem to understand. He said he had been through a lot and needed a drink. I reminded him about the thing coming down from the sky, but he said that wasn't important. He said again that he just needed a drink and walked directly to the bar, grabbed a bottle of whiskey, and started pouring. He repeated the action two or three times, and then he looked at us huddled in the doorway.

He said he had a headache that morning, and it made him want alcohol. He decided to go to St. Michael's, the church outside of town, because any place of God made him want to stay sober.

"Catholic, Lutheran, Baptist, the denomination doesn't matter," he said. "Even a synagogue will do in a pinch."

He started in that direction, but suddenly the storm clouds formed above him, lifted his vehicle from the road, and spun him around one-hundred-and-eighty degrees.

"At that point, I realized a church wasn't going to do it," he said.

He poured himself another glass of whiskey, shrugged his

shoulders, and then looked out the window. Milliken watched the rain fall sideways, the trees bend at forty-degree angles, and a lone car wheel roll down Main Street.

"This is how it's supposed to be when you fall off the wagon," he said as he shrugged his shoulders again. "The world is supposed to end, and everything and everyone you know is supposed to be different."

Pieces of roofing fell onto the concrete, and debris from the street began to swirl in tight circles.

"That's never how it happens though. In fact, it's usually the opposite. You wake up wishing everything changed, but it hasn't. It's all the same, which is why you started drinking in the first place."

Milliken walked near the glass window and saw the funnel descend upon the town. He told me he'd seen a lot of twisters, but nothing like this one. It wasn't from this world. It was from somewhere else.

* * *

It had been coming down hard for days and then weeks. It was the rain from places near the ocean with palm trees and alligators. It was the type that sounds like hail, and the type that scares the hell out of animals. Some of the folks from Sunny Side put on yellow slicks and stood on the side of the highway. They held signs covered with clear plastic trash bags warning about the end of days and demanding repentance for our sins. The rains got so bad that the crops started to drown, and sewage got flushed into the drinking water. The garbage trucks couldn't move through the flooded streets, and the town began to smell. Even the church had a certain odor, and some of the neighbors joked that The Monsignor was storing two of every animal in the utility room behind the sacristy.

After what seemed like forty days the worms finally started to appear, and the rains began to calm. There was an entire army of them, hundreds, thousands, maybe even hundreds of thousands, and they were wiggling in unison. However, the worm child had never seen ones like these. They weren't like the brown ones his dad would put on a hook. They were smaller, fuzzier, and more red. His grandpa once told him that if he dug straight down he'd end up in China, so he figured they must be Chinese worms. He almost always had one in his pocket, along with a little dirt, because he thought there was something lucky about carrying around a worm from China.

* * *

The tornado got closer, and we headed to the cellar. Milliken, however, stayed at the bar. I checked on him after a short while, and I found him dancing around the bar with a Milwaukee's Best ice bucket over his head, proudly singing the ode to the Edmund Fitzgerald. I told him to follow me, but he was barely conscious from all the booze. He slipped on a bar napkin and hit his head on a stool. Some people died that day, but Milliken survived because his brain was covered by ten cents of scrap tin.

We mostly kept old equipment in the cellar, things that we didn't need but didn't want to throw away. Jill and I sat on a full keg, and Milliken used the pony. I caught him looking at some old liquor bottles on the shelf behind me, and I thought he might grab one, but he was too drunk to be sneaky. Plus, he had the bucket on his head, and it would fall over his eyes every time he'd talk or move. I wanted to sober him up, and I thought I might be able to make coffee from the stuff in the cellar.

I found my old Coffee Mate in the corner, and I filled it with water from the janitor's sink. The grounds were in a box that came with the bar, but I figured Milliken wouldn't know any better. I made a makeshift filter from newspaper scraps, and I thought I was in business until I realized the old outlet might not work. I thought about making a battery with the nickels and pennies in my wallet, but luckily the old holes still had power. Then I remembered the Christmas stuff, and found some reindeer mugs behind Biscuits' cat box. I gave Blitzen to Milliken, and I filled it to the top. It smelled like battery acid, but he was too drunk to care.

I didn't have much to say to Milliken. He already drank a bottle of my whiskey, and I didn't like to know too much about the drunks at the bar. Jill, however, seemed curious, and she started asking questions to the man with a bucket on his head.

"Where're you from?" she asked.

"Just up the road."

"You could've gotten killed. You know these storms aren't a joke."

Milliken nodded in agreement, which caused the bucket to pang against the wall behind him.

"I've been trying to get out of this place forever," he mumbled, "but I can't."

"Why do you want to get out?"

"To get away."

"Where do you want to go?"

"No idea."

"How are you going to get there?"

"Walking or driving."

"Well you're too drunk to drive there today."

"Right about that one."

Milliken's eyes began to fade, and his head fell to his lap. I thought he had passed out, but he suddenly sprang to life. Then he asked me to top him off, which I did without delay, and he started talking again.

"I haven't been the same ever since I found that damn Martian rock," he said.

* * *

The worm child would ride his bike to the library and read books about his favorite creatures. He learned that worms were invertebrates, that they lived on land and in water, that there were thirteen phyla, and that the Australian Gippsland, at more than nine feet, is the largest in the world. Robert also learned how to add and maintain nutrients in the soil, to measure moisture levels so they could move with ease, and that the little red worms buried deep in the earth weren't Chinese but either tiger or devil worms. The first are fairly common, the books said, while devil worms are usually found miles below the earth. Tiger worms are more common, so he figured that's what they were, but one of the smaller types was brighter than the others—and they also looked kind of evil—so he told everyone they were devil worms. He explained that devil worms dwell at almost two full miles below the earth, and that some scientists think similar life forms, ones existing far from the sun and deep beneath the ground, may exist on other planets.

* * *

Milliken said it all happened a few years earlier. He bumped into an old timer, Callahan, who said a space ship landed near the railroad tracks on his property. He thought the old man was crazy, but some people heard an explosion that night, and others saw a string of lights in the shape of a triangle. Milliken said people like to make up stories around these parts, but he got to wondering, and he decided to have a look. He waited until late one night, and he snuck onto the old man's land to see if he could find some debris. He brought a flashlight and his boy's red wagon and started scanning the ground.

"I got on my hands and knees and searched every inch along the railroad tracks," Milliken said. "But I didn't find anything until I took a break. I sat down on a rock and realized that it wasn't like any other rock I'd ever seen. It was jagged on all sides, and it had a bunch of little green crystals and crevices. It certainly wasn't from around here, and I was sure that it wasn't from this world."

The bucket once again slipped over Milliken's eyes, but he kept on talking.

"It was three or four times heavier than a normal rock, but I got it in the wagon and rolled it back to the house. I didn't know what it was, and I was scared that someone would take it, so I kept it in my tornado shelter and didn't tell anyone about it. Everyday I'd get off work, pour a drink, and go down into the shelter. The lighting wasn't good, so I installed a string of Christmas lights I had in the attic and one of those giant magnifying glasses people use to tie fishing flies.

"I found a thick book at the library, and I tried to match the pictures and descriptions of the rock with those on the pages. After a week, I confirmed that it wasn't from around here, so I started looking for other books, ones that had more details about rocks from other planets. The pictures in these books looked a lot more like my rock, but there wasn't a perfect match, so I kept looking.

"Then one night I realized there was something growing in one of the crevices. At first, I didn't see it because the substance was small, but I could make it out with the help of the magnifying glass. The next day I found some better lights, took a better look, and I realized it was some type of fungus. From what I knew, nobody had ever found anything alive in outer space, but I wanted to make sure it wasn't something else, so I started getting books on fungi as well.

"The librarian started to take notice of my reading materials, and she asked if I was looking for something. I thought she might think I was crazy, so I just told her I liked collecting rocks. She asked me if I also liked collecting space rocks, probably because I was holding a book on lunar geology, so I smiled and told her it was just a hobby. She told me the answers I was looking for probably weren't in those books, and she suggested I request a book she came across a long time ago.

"She told me she wanted to be an astronomer then, but life happened, and now she was alone with her daughter in a trailer park. I shrugged my shoulders, and she got back on topic, but this time her voice was slightly lower. The librarian told me she and some friends were part of a project, and they once came across a book that might interest me. She said she could help me get it, but it wouldn't be easy. She said that type of knowledge is secret, and that I might need to show some credentials. I told her I could show her plenty of credentials, but they were at home. She smiled at the remark, and she told me I could show them to her over dinner. I wasn't sure if she was interested in me, or if she just wanted to know what I was up to, but I figured I should keep my cards close. Regardless of what happened, her book intrigued me, so I decided to play along."

* * *

Most people think Terrence Heckley was the last person who saw Robert. He lived with his grandma in a small house off Ashton Drive and had been the crossing guard at Hooper Elementary for years. One evening at dinner he told his grandma about a kid who always crossed last when it rained. She asked Terrence why that was, and he said the boy would save the earthworms that washed onto the road. He said Robert would get there around 6 a.m., and that he would slowly move closer to the crosswalk over the course of an hour. Sometimes he would get on his knees, and other times the worm child would stay on foot in his yellow slicks and bend over to get each worm.

Some days Terrence would give Robert a hand. The two rarely talked, but when they did, it was strategy. If Terrence took the ones near the crosswalk, then Robert would get everything south of the schoolyard. If Robert could finish before 6:45, the two of them could clear the walkway together before the bell. One morning after they finished, Terrence asked Robert how many worms he thought he had saved. Probably a million, the worm child responded. He then asked the boy if he would stay out all day if he could, and he said he would, maybe even into the night, because he didn't like being at school, and he didn't like being at home.

* * *

Milliken extended me his mug, but we were out of coffee. I went to fill another pot, and Jill noticed Milliken's wedding ring. She asked if he was wearing it when the librarian asked him to get dinner. He said that he's always worn it because it made him feel like she wasn't gone, like maybe she was just downstairs. Jill asked him why that was: everyone knew she ran off with Carl Buckley, the lawyer. He said it didn't have anything to do with his wife, which Jill didn't really understand, but she decided not to pry. The man was clearly drunk, and she didn't want to squeeze an old trigger.

I brought Milliken a fresh mug. This time it was Donner, and I could tell he was sobering up. He winced at the taste of the coffee, but he kept drinking, maybe to be friendly or maybe just to hold something warm while he told his story.

"We met at the Mexican restaurant known for its enchiladas and green sauce. There were two men seated next to us, both wearing sunglasses that a pilot might wear. The librarian, whose name I still didn't know, sat down in front of me, and she looked nervous. I couldn't tell if it was her first date in a while or if something else was going on. The two men next to us weren't talking, and I wondered if maybe she knew who they were. She looked over her shoulder before telling me I looked nice.

"She said I wasn't like most of the people who came to the library, and I asked why that was. She said most people looked for crime stories, romances, and science fiction. A couple of people look for literature, but it's mostly classics, things they've always meant to read but never did. They just check them out and put them on their coffee table until it's time to return them. In fact, there's a copy of *The Adventures of Huckleberry Finn* that has been checked out seventy-eight times, and she said it doesn't have a single crease, stain, or dog ear.

"I asked her what she made of it, and she just shrugged, saying she wasn't sure what it meant, but that it must mean something.

"I nodded, but I was more focused on the man with sunglasses.

He was sliding his chair a few inches closer to the table, maybe to overhear what we were saying.

"I looked at him to show that I knew what he was up to, and he immediately lifted his chin to give the impression that he was looking at something over my head. He then scratched his nose and took a long drink of water from a glass that appeared to be empty. Then he took another drink, maybe to convince me there was something in his glass or to send a signal to someone else. The other man, whose face I couldn't see, kept scratching behind his hat, which made me think he was nervous or mouthing a message to his partner.

"The librarian continued by saying the book was something special, but that she couldn't tell me about it here. I asked her why that was, and she said it was better to go somewhere private, somewhere away from prying eyes.

"Then she raised her right eyebrow, lowered her chin, and gestured her head in the direction of the men seated behind her, as if to indicate they were listening to us. I wasn't sure though, so I tested my theory by raising my right eyebrow and winking with my left eye. The purpose was to show the woman that I was following her suggestions, but she seemed confused. I did it again, this time a little more exaggerated, and she asked if there was something wrong with my eye.

"Before I knew it the food arrived. The smell of cheese, cilantro, and sauce left an impression on the librarian, who closed her eyes and seemed to be carried away by the aroma. We must have both been hungry because we didn't say a word for a few minutes. We just worked our way through the beans, rice, and pork wrapped in flour tortillas. Mine were a little too spicy for my usual taste, but it didn't bother me like it would have on other nights.

"Then I noticed one of the men, the one with his back to us, use his index finger to trace a line from the surface of the table to a specific point in the air above his shoulder. It looked like he was signaling a direction or perhaps tracing the movement of a meteorite. It was strange the two of them weren't eating, as the place was well known for its enchiladas, and I wondered what other reason they would have for being in a restaurant at dinner time. More importantly, I wondered why they were seated next to us in a room that was almost completely empty.

"She then whispered that we should finish our dinner. I nodded and asked for the check, and the men were gone before it arrived. I didn't see or hear them get up because I was too busy studying the librarian, who had lit a cigarette she had retrieved from her purse. She smoked half of it and then used her side of refried beans as an ashtray. I left a couple of bills on the table, and she took my hand on the way out. She whispered, 'I have something for you,' as we exited, but I no longer had any idea of what she was implying."

* * *

The children ran frantically through the storm, and they didn't follow the crossing guard's instructions. The Platte swelled, and the water in Thompson Creek began to overflow. They should have closed the old bridge earlier that morning, but the city workers were known for being slow. Parents didn't know their kids took the shortcut over the bridge in the park to get to school. The wood bent beneath the children's boots as they crossed, but they were unaware of the dangers, laughing and skipping in brightly colored rain jackets through the thick sheets of rain. The worms were piling on the sidewalk, and Terrence wondered why the worm child wasn't working. He asked the other kids where Robert was, and some said he was at the basketball court near the park bridge.

Terrence followed the street past the church, down Workman Avenue, and then took the shortcut down the hill where the kids would reconnect with the main street. Terrence said the waters from the Platte that fed into the creek upstream had completely flooded over, and the current churned down Thomp-

son Creek, pulling chunks of earth, low-hanging branches, and stolen shopping carts down the way. Terrence stepped onto the bridge and realized it was going to collapse. Then he noticed an opening in the middle. He said it was about twice the size of an ice fishing hole.

He noticed there wasn't a single worm on the surface leading up to the hole, and even Terrence seemed to know what that meant. He started to walk back to school, but he noticed something strange about the basketball court and started running toward it. He said he almost slipped on the surface because the rain was still coming down so hard, but he eventually arrived at half court and observed Robert's greatest feat. The entire playing surface was covered with leaves, puddles, and acorns, but it was completely devoid of worms. Terrence then recalled with great enthusiasm how the court had always been saturated with the tiny creatures when it would rain. He said it wasn't a matter of a hundred or two; he said there were probably millions. He said Robert not only saved all the worms that afternoon, but he had placed them in a pile that reached as high as the rim of the basket. He said it was the worm child's greatest accomplishment, a monument to himself and the creatures that he loved.

* * *

"The walk back to the house was long, but it was a nice evening, so we took our time. It had been a while since I had talked to a woman, and I liked how she was interested in space and other things beyond our world. She told me to wait on her porch as she ran into her house. She returned with a book, kissed me on the cheek, and said goodnight.

"I ran to the shelter once the door closed. Maybe it was a once-in-a-lifetime discovery, I thought. Maybe it was proof life existed elsewhere. Maybe it proved we weren't monkeys but aliens from a meteorite from a planet with no name. Maybe they'll name it after me. Milliken they'll call it. No, that doesn't sound right.

They'll have to throw a bunch of numbers after it. Milliken #758. Yeah. That sounds about right.

"The proxy light was on when I got back to the house. I figured a raccoon had set it off, but the front door was open. I ran inside, and it looked like a tornado had blown through. Someone had gone through my desk, my library books on the shelf, and someone took a crowbar to the drawer where I kept my old mail. Everything in the house was still there, so they weren't looking for money. I thought about the two men sitting next to us at dinner, and I figured I must have come up on a list. And the librarian? She was probably involved. They probably told her to find me at the library, find out who I was, and then distract me so they could move in.

"I ran outside, and the proxy light turned on again, but this time my attention was focused on the shelter. The door that led into the ground was shattered into pieces."

* * *

The sheriff had his own theory about what happened. Everyone knew that Milliken's wife left him, and that he liked to drink. She left town and then tried to get custody with the lawyer. It wasn't hard because Milliken was a lousy father. He mostly ignored his son, and the worm child would play outside by himself when his dad was at home. The boy would usually be seen alone on the swing set, riding his bike, or reading about worms on the porch. The neighbors even told a story about the time they saw the boy at the library. They were returning some books one day when they noticed Robert alone at a table reading. They asked him how he was doing, but he stayed quiet and avoided eye contact.

The neighbor woman asked him why he was reading about worms, but the boy stayed quiet. Finally, she told Robert he could talk to her and that she would keep his secret. She asked why he wanted to save the worms, but again, he didn't reply. Finally, after a few minutes of silence, she said the boy closed the book he was reading, reached into his pocket, and pulled out a clump of wet soil and an enormous knot of earthworms. After that, he reached his other hand into his other pocket and did the same. He showed her both masses of earth and worms and then put them on the table. He wiped the mud and residue on his pants, which she said hadn't been washed in a while, and then Robert stuck his hands back in his pockets. "I like them because they stay hidden," he said. "They don't want to come to the surface, but they can't help it. I put them back in the mud so nobody can hurt them."

Milliken lost custody, but he could still see him every couple of weeks. Things went well for a while: the mom's car would pull into the driveway, Robert would get out, and she would be back the following Sunday morning, just in time for church. During the week, Robert usually played by himself in the garden. He also rescued worms on the sidewalk or he would ride his bike up and down the road toward St. Michael's. People in town saw them when Milliken would take the boy to get lunch or dinner at the bar. They would also see him finish a pitcher or two before driving his son home.

After Robert disappeared, the sheriff started following Milliken. He also questioned him to see if his story held up. Milliken always said he was at work when the boy disappeared. He drove for a landscape supplies company, and his time sheets verified parts of the story, but the records showed that it took him almost two hours longer than usual to drop off some pesticides that day. Milliken said he had stopped for gas, that the line was long, and that he had paid for the fuel in cash. The sheriff pulled the security cameras from the gas station, but the owner hadn't replaced the battery. As the weeks went on, Milliken quit showing up at work and dedicated himself to drinking. He also started visiting the library. He may have been looking for his son, but he was checking out strange books about the universe, some of which were tagged.

* * *

I expected my windows to be blown out, my glassware shattered, and the roof to be gone. Most of that didn't happen, though. There was just a lot of broken glass from a tree that had fallen through the window facing the street. It was resting on the booth against the wall facing west, and I told Jill it probably needed a drink. She didn't like the joke and said it would be expensive, but I promised the insurance would take care of it. I even wondered if it could be good for business—you know, come in and drink with a tree. I could even serve custom cocktails: Falling Maples, Squirrel Shooters—maybe tell people they get a free drink if they're older than its rings.

Jill and I grabbed a broom, and Milliken found a pan. We started piling debris in the corner, and it was about chest-high when someone came to see if we were open. I told the guy to beat it, but then another person came by, and I told him to grab a seat wherever he wanted. Milliken took my broom, and I opened the bar. The place was soon packed with people telling stories about what happened. Their voices got louder around dusk, and the people started talking in one large group. And, like usual, the topic turned to Sunny Side. A tornado wiped most of them out a while ago, but the survivors rebuilt the property and continued preaching their ways.

They believe in a book that talks about how aliens come to earth every hundred years and take their most loyal followers. Apparently, there's a chapter that describes the location of a landing zone, which they believe is on an energy field near the railroad tracks on Callahan's property. And, to their credit, strange things do happen around here. Floods and tornados seem to hit Hooper worse than other places, and people are always talking about crop circles and bright lights on the highway.

The people at Sunny Side believe the aliens will make them kings, queens, and whatever else of their planet. They also said their ideas were backed by science, which is why they were always at the library. Some of the members even started working there, and they opened a new wing with strange reading material. One day people showed up in suits and were flashing badges, and they said certain books were no longer available in this particular library. They said a few other books were tagged, and anyone who requested them might be questioned by specified, unnamed officials. When that tornado hit, however long ago that was, it touched down directly on the Sunny Side Trailer park, and people in town joked that the cult finally got its wish. All the believers were taken into the sky.

Later, people said men in strange suits were checking out the Sunny Side property. Some said they were picking things up and putting them into silver garbage bags, but others said they worked for the city, or the county, or whatever. From there, more rumors began to fly. One woman said the tornado was a portal for the cult to access the other side, and a drunk farmer even showed me a piece of paper his grandson found on his property. He said it was probably from one of the books about aliens, but he said not to tell anyone because he figured the men in suits would come and take it.

Everyone shuffled out around ten. I locked the bar, even though it still had a tree through the middle of it, and I started walking home. I thought Milliken was moving in the other direction, but I soon realized he was following me. He had waited for everyone to leave because he wanted to tell me something important. I told him we should probably talk about it in the morning, but he insisted we go back to his place.

"This is important," he said.

We walked carefully around fallen power lines until we arrived at Milliken's house. The lights didn't work, so we sat at his kitchen table in the dark. He asked if I wanted a drink, and I told him I'd take a beer if he had one. He said he didn't have any, but he offered me a whiskey. He had a warm, half-drank bottle of his favorite stuff, and I told him to forget it. He poured himself a water glass full of the brown liquid, took a long drink, and then sat down next to me.

"I didn't tell you the truth," he said.

Milliken was drunk, but his eyes were sharp.

"Those guys who busted through here. They weren't just looking for some space rock. They were looking for something else. I found some bodies on that land, and they weren't from around here. They were badly burned and mutilated, but I managed to fit them in my wheel barrel."

Milliken returned to his bottle of whiskey on the counter, poured another glass, and drank it in a single gulp. He tried to stumble back to his seat, but he fell on the floor. I tried to help him up, but I could only get his front half pulled over the chair. He looked me straight in the eyes and cleared his throat.

"They got the rock, but they didn't get the bodies. I buried them out back under the woodpile."

Milliken then passed out, and I walked to the back porch. There was a storage bin near the door, and I found an old flashlight with a weak beam that flickered when you moved it. Then I opened the door, and the proxy light went on. The power was out everywhere else in the county, but Milliken's porch shone brightly for almost an acre. It was raining lightly, and the drops had washed several earthworms near my feet. Then I looked to my right and saw a shovel resting on the side of the house. I lightly beat it against the patio to remove the dirt caked to the metal.

The proxy light reset as I stepped onto his land. The woodpile was a few yards outside the fence that marked his property. I jumped the barrier and approached the mess of twigs and branches. Then I removed a wood stump, placed it beside the pile, and rested the flashlight on it so I could see what I was doing. I began moving sticks and logs with the shovel until I finally reached the ground. Then I wondered if Milliken had brought me there on purpose. I wondered if the tornado was part of something bigger, and I wondered if Robert had existed at all.

The proxy light then went off, and I stood near the flickering bulb that illuminated the work area. I slid the shovel into the wet soil, and dozens of earthworms came up in a single scoop. I threw them to the side, and then slid the metal end back into the ground.

I repeated the action until the worms turned smaller and redder. Then the light started to dim, and soon I was standing in a dark hole. I took a break to wipe the rain and sweat off my forehead, and I thought about quitting, but the light suddenly returned. It was brighter than before, and I decided to take one more swipe. I put both hands on the shovel and slammed it into the soil with the little energy left in my arms. I hit something hard that cracked on contact, and I wondered if Robert was where he wanted to be, finally alone with the worms.

"Chief" (Part I)

Chief arrived in Baxter County the fall before the twister. He was Chief on the reservation near Baxter County and later worked as a Chief of Police outside Indie, but he started driving a semi-trailer after his mother died. For years, he saw everything on the road: head-on collisions, crop duster accidents, and even a chupacabra. One day, Chief stopped at a park and noticed some guys throwing a ball and driving one another into the ground. They were big like him and laughed as they crashed their enormous bodies and bled from their heads. After a few hours, Chief was laughing and bleeding alongside them, and the guys asked if he wanted to join their rugby team. They were headed to a tournament in Wales, and they needed someone with his size and power.

Chief said he didn't have any money and didn't know where Wales was on a map. They said Wales was near England, and he didn't have to worry about the money. Chief left his truck somewhere on the East Coast and got on a plane the next day. He ran, hit, and kicked like a moose, and the team went undefeated. His play caught the attention of professional teams in the area, and he got calls from recruiters when he returned home. A club in Edinburgh was ready to fly him in for a tryout, but his truck jack-knifed before he left. The doctors put Chief back together, but he couldn't play like before. He moved back to the reservation to live with family and took odd jobs when he was healthy enough to work.

Chief got his break one afternoon when he was approached by an aging man with a gun, a limp, and a badge. Sheriff Hardy told Chief he was going to retire soon, and the lawman said he had heard about his work in Indie. He told Chief he could train him on the job, and he'd be ready by spring. Chief admitted that he'd been arrested a few times when he was younger, but the sheriff just shrugged his shoulders.

"The job is yours if you want it."

* * *

Chief took his first call in early spring. Dispatch said it was Nana, who everyone in town called "El Diablo." Nana never showed up to court for a disturbance at a bar, and there was a warrant out for his arrest. Sheriff Hardy tried to book him for punching a man in the face at Al's, but Nana wasn't going to prison without a fight. He broke the old lawman's nose, and nobody saw Nana again until he resurfaced a year later at the same bar in Hooper. The station said he needed to be arrested that evening, but Chief said he'd do it in the morning. The woman at the station insisted he do it that night because Nana would probably be drinking and stir up trouble. She also said he should bring backup. El Diablo stood almost seven feet tall and could punch a hole through a brick wall, but Chief told her not to worry about it. He said he knew where to find Nana, and that he'd take care of it in the morning.

Chief woke early the next day, put on his badge, and headed to Peg's Diner. He knew that's where Nana liked to cure his hangovers, but this morning El Diablo looked sober. He wasn't causing trouble, just eating eggs and toast. There were only a few people at Peg's that morning, and their eyes moved away from the headlines as Chief approached Nana at the bar and took a seat.

"Are you Nana?" he asked.

The man looked at him, and then kept eating his eggs.

"You know there's a warrant out for your arrest?"

The man shrugged.

"Well," Chief said. "I'm going to get some coffee, and you finish your eggs, and when we're done, we'll get this taken care of."

Chief put his hat on the bar, ordered his coffee black, and then asked Nana for the sports section. El Diablo looked confused and asked why he wasn't taking him to jail right then.

"No reason to waste good eggs," Chief said. "I can't work before my coffee, anyway."

Chief soon ordered a side of bacon. The two men split it, along with the business section. Peg came by and topped them off a second time, but Chief said it was time for a switch.

"Decaf is for warm-ups," he said with a wink.

Peg grabbed the pot with the green top and refilled Chief's coffee. Then she topped off El Diablo.

"What happened to the other sheriff?" Nana asked.

"He's probably at Mel's," he said. "He doesn't like the coffee here, even though it's the same. Anyway, it doesn't matter. He retired a while ago."

"Where'd you come from?"

"A reservation not far from here."

"Better for you. People around here aren't right. They look normal, but they aren't. There's always something wrong with them."

Chief smiled at the woman from dispatch when they arrived at the station. She was concerned that Nana wasn't cuffed, but Chief told her not to worry. He said they were all adults, and there wasn't any reason to get excited.

"Nana just has to make a call."

An hour later an older woman arrived at the precinct with some money. Chief assumed it was Nana's mother, but he didn't ask who it was, or where she had gotten the cash for bail. Chief told Nana he didn't want to see him at the precinct again, and that he'd drop the charges if he kept his nose clean for the rest of the year. Otherwise, he was going to the prison outside Davenport, the bad one where they kept the real criminals. As Nana walked out the door, Chief repeated that he didn't want to see him at the precinct again, but it'd be fine if he saw him at Peg's.

* * *

Not long after, Chief got a call about a man named Hank Berry. A highway patrolman had pulled into town to fill up on gas and saw Hank on the road with a weapon walking on the road not far from Baxter Community College. Chief already knew Hank from other calls. He was a middle-aged alcoholic who stayed sober until Thursday. One night a week he liked to get loaded, walk home, and cause trouble on the way. Hank was a nuisance, but he wasn't dangerous, and Chief couldn't imagine him carrying a weapon. He told the patrolman he'd take care of it, but the man insisted that he should provide backup. He said his name was Officer Lang, and Chief agreed to let him tag along under one condition: the patrolman had to stay in his car.

Officer Lang picked up Chief at the precinct. Chief closed the car door, removed his belt with the gun, and threw it in the back seat.

"That'll only complicate things," Chief said.

Officer Lang shrugged and turned up the music. It was a song Chief had never heard, and one he didn't care for.

"I like to play country when I got the black boys in the back," the patrolman said.

Chief remained quiet. Then he reminded the patrolman of their agreement.

"I don't care what happens. This is my town, and you take orders from me."

The patrolman didn't respond, so Chief repeated his directions. Officer Lang nodded and then pulled to the side of the road, about a dozen feet from where Hank was standing.

Chief got out of the car, approached Hank, and told him to show his hands. The man didn't follow directions, however, and instead jumped into the irrigation ditch beside the road and then disappeared into a cornfield. Then Officer Lang told Chief to get his gun because they were going after him, but Chief said no. He said to be patient.

"Hank's no pheasant," the sheriff said. "Give him ten minutes in that corn maze, and he'll turn right back around."

The patrolman insisted they go after him, but Chief told him to turn off his car, stay seated, and be quiet.

Soon they heard a rumbling, and Chief yelled into the corn. He told Hank there was no reason to spend the night in jail, and that he'd take him home if he came out. He said they could keep the whole thing between the two of them, but he just had to come out of that cornfield.

"You promise?" Hank asked.

"I don't go back on my word," Chief responded.

"Alright then."

The two only waited a few minutes before Hank reappeared. His left hand was on his hip, and his right hand was in his pocket. Chief asked him to show his hands, but he didn't respond.

"Lousy drunk's got a gun," the patrolman said from the car.

Officer Lang's voice made Hank agitated. He yelled something incoherent, but Chief told him to stay calm.

"Just show your hands so we know you aren't causing any trouble," Chief repeated.

The sheriff then heard the car door open, and his eyes flashed back to the vehicle.

"You stay in that damn car, Lang."

The patrolman got out, removed his flashlight, and directed the beam at Hank's face.

"Turn that damn thing off," he told the patrolman. "You're spooking him."

Then he looked back at Hank.

"I promise you won't spend the night in jail if you show me your hands," Chief said.

The patrolman didn't listen to Chief and put his hand on his gun.

"No more games," the patrolman said. "I'm counting right now, and you better have both your hands on the ground before I count to three."

Chief crossed his arms and told Officer Lang he was making a big mistake.

"Nobody has to die tonight."

"1 . . . "

Chief thought about tackling the patrolman, but Lang saw what he was thinking. He turned the gun on Chief and told him to get in the car.

"I'm taking things from here," he said.

Chief looked at the man carefully. His mouth and fingers were twitching, and he was frantically turning the gun between him and Hank.

"Slow down," Chief said. "And put the gun down. Nobody has to die tonight."

The officer closed his eyes, took a breath, and started to put his gun down. He seemed calmer when he reopened them, but Hank took his hand out of his pocket. Chief didn't know what he was holding, but it didn't matter. Officer Lang pulled the trigger three times, and Hank fell dead on the concrete. Chief radioed for an ambulance as the patrolman got back into his car. He said he just got a call elsewhere and disappeared into an empty highway surrounded by ditches and cornfields.

Chief kneeled next to the body and opened Hank's right hand. He found an object, but it wasn't a knife, and it certainly wasn't a gun.

Professor Williams

Professor Williams had an office that looked like a yard sale. She was in her fifth year at Baxter Community College, and in that time, she had accumulated a decade of papers, folders, textbooks, and cardboard boxes that were organized in piles covered with sticky notes and dust bunnies. She swore there was an unseen order to the madness, but visitors had to step around piles of library books, wire sculptures of Don Quixote, rogue crayons, and outstanding poster presentations from the previous decade. Some would also notice the slight change in smell. It was not a foul odor, per say, but it was different from the rest of the Department of Modern Languages.

While waiting for Professor Williams to arrive late to a departmental meeting that day, Professor Isakov swore to his colleagues he once saw a mouse run out of a yogurt cup on her desk and ascend—via a cardboard tube for carrying maps—to the third level of her bookshelf. From there, he said the small, white creature entered a crease between the 1985 edition of *La Real Academia Española* and the *Complete Works of Spanish Postwar*

Theater. Everyone knew the scenario was plausible, and even the department chair—a late-aged German woman named Professor Brugenheimer—remarked that she too had seen something move in Professor Williams' office one day, but ultimately decided not to investigate. They joked about using department funds for mouse traps when their colleague finally arrived.

Professor Brugenheimer opened the meeting with that week's bureaucratic order: distribution of the agenda, review of the previous week's minutes, request to approve the previous week's minutes, and the presentation of topics for the current meeting. The group had already voted to approve the minutes when Professor Jiménez—who actually taught French—noticed an error in the previous week's notes. She was known for her redacting skills and on one occasion had successfully impeded the approval process for a memorable twenty-eight minutes. Today, the revision was quick but could not have been worthier of her attention. Last week Professor Williams and Professor Rivera had petitioned for $100 to purchase a button-maker. The junior faculty explained how other departments had stirred interest and attracted majors by creating personalized buttons students could proudly wear on their backpacks. Fun slogans like "Bio Nerd" and "Book Worm" yielded an identity for Biology and English majors, while the more daring "hard scientist" and "Phy*sexual*" attracted the attention of science majors, department chairs, and the dean of students.

Unfortunately, the idea was quickly vanquished. The senior faculty were always in the majority and strictly enforced any changes that could threaten *their life work*. But again, the pause was not because of the request for a button maker—Professor Jiménez had already put an end to *that idea*—it was the result of Professor Isakov's imprecision with the prepositions *in* and *on*. He had erroneously typed that students could wear the buttons *in* their bags and not *on* their bags, which, Professor Jiménez noted, would have invalidated the original purpose of the buttons and the entire paragraph. The rest of the room confirmed or pretended to confirm the mistake, and the elderly French professor once again evinced her cognitive prowess to those colleagues who thought she should have retired at 70.

With the correction made, Professor Brugenheimer advanced the agenda and shared the order of topics for the meeting: solutions to low enrollment, awards for current majors, summer teaching positions, and the tenure of Professor Williams. Unfortunately, Dr. Jiménez's digression had opened the door to Dr. Isakov, who was well into his sixties and wanted to make up for his grammatical indiscretion by observing a mistake of his own. The Russian professor noted an error in the description of the process by which students were asked about applying for study abroad. At the previous meeting the faculty had decided to formulate a "questionnaire" that students would have to complete in order to go on Professor Williams' trip to Costa Rica, but the keen eye of Dr. Isakov was not convinced.

"In reality it isn't a questionnaire," he told his colleagues.

"And then what is it?" asked Professor Jiménez.

"It is a document with a series of questions."

Professor Williams' eyes moved to Professor Rivera, who had begun picking at a stubborn piece of glue on the table. Then she peered at the clock. The weekly meeting was only supposed to last thirty minutes, from 4-4:30, but it always exceeded an hour. The only topic of interest was buried at the end, and she estimated they wouldn't get to it until at least 5:00. Worst of all, she had made plans to meet with Professor McKendrick near the planetarium at 5:30. She was hoping there would be time to run home before they went for a drink. She wanted to talk to him about something important tonight, and she wanted more time to pull her thoughts together. Unfortunately, it looked like she would be arriving late to that meeting as well.

The discussion progressed to summer teaching sometime around 5:00, but the sound of sirens became a distraction. Professor Rivera said he remembered talk of severe weather and volunteered to take a look. Professor Williams watched him remove a pack of cigarettes from his pocket as he exited the room, and she might have volunteered to join him, but they were nearing the discussion of her promotion.

Professor Williams had been patient in her dealings with colleagues and stayed focused on the future. Soon she and Professor Rivera would be able to make changes the department and the college desperately needed. Unfortunately, her superiors continued to delay retirement, so she would often fantasize about the years to come. She imagined attractive men in blue uniforms who would be called in to remove the bodies of her coworkers as they fell—one by one—from natural causes in their offices and classrooms. During some faculty meetings she could even see the looks of horror and fascination on the faces of students as their professors disappeared beneath a bag and the sound of a zipper.

The voice of Dr. Rivera and the smell of burned tobacco interrupted Professor Brugenheimer as she announced the discussion of tenure for Professor Williams. Professor Rivera said that everyone had to get home *right now* because something big was about to hit. At this point, Professor Brugenheimer decided to adjourn the meeting and leave the last topic of discussion for the following week. Professor Williams could not hide her frustration, but nobody seemed to notice as her colleagues frantically headed for the parking lot. Professor Williams was still seated at her desk when the last person exited. It was Professor Rivera, and he looked back and said "I'm sorry, Linda" before the door shut behind him.

Professor Williams remained in her chair and noticed a similar piece of hardened glue not unlike the one Professor Rivera had discovered. She started picking at it, but her finger slipped, and it removed a small line of polish from her thumbnail.

"Joder," she said.

It was already 5:28, and it was time to meet Professor McKendrick at the planetarium. She wasn't going to let a tornado interfere with her date, but she wasn't sure her partner would feel the same. She walked past the large window near the stairwell that led to the exit, and a loud rumble soon brought her attention to the approaching storm. She decided to call Professor McKendrick, but he did not answer. She hung up, called again, and then left a message asking him to meet her in the Modern Languages Building. She began to think about her message, but a man's voice interrupted her as he approached from the hallway. He was very tall, had turtle-framed glasses, and was holding a copy of *The Groves of Acadame.*

"Professor Williams, I'm glad I caught you. I needed to ask . . . "

"Professor Schraeder, what are you doing here? Don't you know what's going on out there?"

"Out there? What do you mean?"

"The storm, Professor Schraeder. There's a tornado on the way. Look out the window."

"A tornado? My gosh."

"So maybe you should go home, Professor Schraeder?"

"Home? Well, you see Professor Williams, I walked here today."

"Follow me out, Professor Schraeder," she said. "I'll give you a ride."

"But I really should get my . . . "

"We're leaving now."

Professor Williams gave Professor Schraeder her bag and told him to follow. His legs were much larger than hers, but he had trouble keeping up. The two moved down the hallway, descended the stairwell, and walked swiftly toward the exit.

She opened the door with a thrust of her hips and was met with a cold gust of wind that blew her back into the building. The door slammed shut, and for the first time Professor Schraeder seemed aware of the danger.

"Gosh, I've never seen a tornado before."

"We're fine, Professor Schraeder. It's just April in the Midwest. The storm will blow over the college, and the tornado, if there even is one, will take out a bunch of corn silos in the middle of nowhere. If anything, we should be happy. It's the only time this college makes the news."

"I guess we'll be here for a while," he said.

"Yeah, I guess so. We should probably get to the shelter."

"At least I brought my book."

"Great, you can tell me about it while we're down there."

They descended two flights of stairs that led to a subterranean hallway. The sign on the door read "Tornado and Bomb Shelter," but it was locked. Professor Williams removed her key ring, which actually consisted of four rings and about two dozen keys.

"Maybe I missed my calling," Professor Williams said. "I should have been a janitor."

Professor Schraeder did not hear the joke or perhaps he did not understand it. He smiled because it seemed like she was saying something funny, and he wanted to be supportive.

The key was the smallest on the ring, and it was hidden between the one for the supply closet in 3A and the one for the overhead projector in room 4B. The hallway was lit with dim emergency lighting and was covered with old pipes and pink insulation that looked like cotton candy. There were no chairs, so the two sat on the floor with their backs against a cement wall.

Professor Schraeder positioned himself directly beneath one of the emergency lights to read. Professor Williams was impressed by his calmness. He was a curious man whose height, well over six feet, made him look like an athlete, but she could not imagine him jogging, catching a ball, or even wearing shorts. He was an excellent researcher, but it was difficult for him to interact with people outside his field. The key to colleagues like Professor Schraeder, she knew, was to ask specific questions about specific topics, namely his research.

"So what are you reading, Professor Schraeder?"

He waited a moment, possibly to finish a sentence from the book, and then looked at his colleague.

"I'm sorry Professor Williams, did you ask me something?"

"I did. What are you reading?"

"Oh, well, you see, it's an academic novel."

"Can you tell me about it?"

"About the book I'm reading or the academic novel in general?"

"Aren't they the same thing?"

Professor Schraeder chuckled. This was his type of humor: duplicity and incongruence.

"Well, this is an iteration of the genre we call the academic novel, and an important one at that. It is from the 1950s, and many say it is the first one ever written."

"What is it . . . or . . . they about?"

"Many things," he said. "These are novels about students who deal with difficult professors, professors dealing with colleagues and tenure, and there is also a lot of, how do I say it, *intrigue*."

His smile extended to both ears.

"Well, in all truth, there isn't much of that in this particular work, but there are others, ones that are a bit more recent and, how do I say it, less *highbrow*. They have some very *intri-*, that is, captivating storylines."

"Like what?" Professor Williams asked.

There is one about a young professor who is trying to get tenure.

"Oh yeah?"

"Oh yes, it is a young woman in fact who is dealing with some very difficult colleagues. Some of them are a bit too set in their ways to welcome a new member to the department.

"What happens?"

"Well, the young professor is ultimately denied tenure and must learn to live outside Academia."

"And does she?"

"Well, she has a tough go with things. She is denied work at all the other universities, and soon decides to spend a day with her sister in another state, who is a high school teacher there. Her sister is more traditional, and the two of them argue about the importance of having children. She does not want to be like her sister in any way, and so she decides high school is not for her.

"So, what does she do?"

"Well . . . she ends up in prison."

"What?"

"She ultimately decides to murder the aging French professor who was the definitive vote against her tenure. It's something of a happy ending, though, because she explains at the end that the only place for a professor outside academe is an asylum or a prison.

"What else have you read?"

"Well there's another one about . . . *an affair.*"

"Sounds adult."

"Quite. It is about a middle-aged female student who starts taking classes after a divorce and eventually pursues a relationship with her history professor.

"At first, the professor is distant, but she is persistent and comes to his office hours several times a week. Unfortunately, she is not a particularly gifted pupil, and the professor thinks that she is not a good mate."

"So, what happens?"

"Well, over time the two find connections that bring them together outside the classroom. The two of them enjoy the sport of softball, for example, and by engaging in these and other activities he begins to see her as a person and not just a student."

"So, they live happily ever after?"

"Quite the contrary. The administration eventually learns about their extracurricular activities when a photo of them—quite drunk and clearly in love—surfaces on campus.

"The professor is denied tenure, and months later she is no longer interested in him. He comes to her door one evening a little drunk to ask her to marry him, but the woman's ex-husband answers the door. The two exchange words, and soon they are fighting. The ex-husband pummels the ex-professor with blows, and he is left bleeding and unconscious on the woman's lawn."

"Sounds terrible."

"Indeed. The next morning, she finds the professor in the grass and realizes he is dead."

"Do any of these stories have a happy ending?"

"Well, there is a new author I recently read, but his work is quite strange. His is a story about a young female professor in the humanities who works at a small liberal arts college in the Midwest, and she falls for a slightly older male professor from another department, something in science. Anyway, they meet at a faculty engagement and share a connection with their love of science fiction and the idea of time travel. The two decide to meet for coffee later that day, but the male professor eventually cancels. A few weeks later she bumps into him at a poetry reading she has organized for her students at a coffee shop. The two once again share a connection, and they decide to have a drink afterward. They share a marvelous night that ends in her bedroom, but the science professor never returns her calls.

"While this is going on, she is also in the final phase of her tenure review and is dealing with a difficult colleague who is trying to deny her promotion. Furthermore, she is struggling with a male student who constantly contradicts her in class. She confronts the student one day, and he eventually apologizes and says his behavior was out of line. In the following weeks, things begin to go the professor's way. The student completely changes his behavior and becomes more engaged in class. The two slowly develop a friendship, and she learns that he is the darling of the Physics department. He writes her a glowing recommendation that catches the attention of the dean and the chancellor, and she begins to suspect that tenure is inevitable. Moreover, the nasty colleague who had been rallying support against her falls ill and is forced to take medical leave for the rest of the academic year.

"That weekend she celebrates her success. She leaves the small town, Buxton I believe it was called, and goes out in the big city. She meets up with girlfriends, and they begin to drink and dance at an establishment she frequented in her younger years. She soon goes to the bar to order a drink and notices the science professor in the corner with another woman. She thinks about approaching them but decides it better to return to her friends and watch the two from afar. The girl is younger than her, has darker hair, and some features she fears may be more impressive than her own. Time passes, and she eventually watches the woman get up from the table and go to the bar. The woman decides to do the same, and she is surprised to see that the girl with the male professor is actually one of her students.

"The student, Darcy, had been one of the professor's favorite pupils. She took the professor's Composition I class during her freshman year and had decided to become an English major on her recommendation. The two had worked closely on creative writing projects and analytical papers, and she not only told Darcy she should go on to graduate school but that the young woman's writing often reminded her of her own.

"The professor decides to buy Darcy a drink, and while they are in line she admits that she has been watching her with Dr. Russford. Darcy simpers at the revelation, but her professor tells her not to worry. She says they are both consenting adults, and she should not feel embarrassed. After all, she says with a smile, it's not like it's an older female professor and a younger male student.

"Darcy soon goes to the restroom, and the professor approaches Dr. Russford alone at the table. She does not say a word but takes the cardboard coaster from beneath his drink, flips it around, and writes the name of a bar on the back. She says goodbye to her friends and takes a cab home. Before she leaves, however, she lets the bouncer know there is an adult male buying drinks for a minor at the table at the back of the bar.

"It is still relatively early when she returns to town and has a nightcap at a place where the students aren't welcome. It is a townie bar called The Irishman, and it is mostly inhabited with drunks and hipsters. She orders a scotch because it seems to fit the setting, and she stares into the glass as she waits. She looks around the room and mostly notices alcoholics also gazing into their drinks or at themselves in the half-empty liquor bottles behind the bar.

"There is, however, a person who does not fit in. It is a young man working on some type of math problem directly under a small lamp with a green cover that is attached to the wall. He looks like someone she knows, but her interest is interrupted by the bartender, who asks if she wants another drink. She nods in agreement and then looks back at the young man, who is none other than her student, the star of the Physics department. The drink arrives, and she brings it over to his table. She asks him what he's doing there, and he says he could ask her the same thing. At that point, she tells him to call her Linda, and he says he was going to but wasn't sure if he should. She then asks him why he's studying at a place like this, and he says it's better than a library because nobody ever talks. Plus, there's alcohol.

"The professor is impressed by his logic and asks him what he's working on. He says it is a formula he is developing with Dr. Russford. He says they are trying to describe the world, or at least a small piece of it. He tells her they want to understand the order of the world outside our brains, but she tells him that it is impossible because he is using his brain to figure it out. The professor goes on, saying that it sounds like he is describing a way for humans to understand nature, and by doing so, they are defining it in their own terms. The student says he had never thought of it that way, and he wonders what Dr. Russford might say.

"The two drop the larger questions of the universe and order another drink. At this point the student admits that he is fascinated by the idea of time travel, and that his real desire is to discover a formula that describes how it might work. She seems skeptical of the idea but admits that such a formula would benefit humanity. He asks her why she thinks that, and she says that we deserve the right to enjoy our mistakes without the burden of consequences. Before she can continue, however, he asks if all mistakes are errors or if some are just explained that way later. She smiles at the idea and notices that her student has placed his hand on her leg. The professor is certain that Dr. Russford will soon be at the bar, but she decides to take her new friend to her apartment for one last drink."

"Wait a minute," Professor Williams interrupts. "I thought you said this story had a happy ending."

"Just a little more patience," Professor Schraeder said. "The night proceeds just as you would expect it to, and word soon gets out about their *affair*. The campus community, especially its elders, cite her *turpitude* as a blatant violation of the sacred teacher-student relationship. She is denied tenure and is forced to move to another town. She takes a job at a coffee shop and uses the energy from her frustrations to write novels. She produces three of them in one year and becomes a bestselling author. Her most famous novel is her first, *The Position of the Matriarch*, which tells the heartbreaking story of a female professor who is unfairly accused of having a relationship with a student. And, of course, the character uses her frustration to begin a new career as a writer."

"I like the story," Professor Williams said. "But it doesn't seem believable."

"You must remember," Professor Schraeder responded with a smile. "This is not reality. It is fiction."

With that, Professor Schraeder put down his book and walked toward the door. He said he should check the weather, but Professor Williams remained on the floor contemplating the stories the man had told her. Professor Williams wondered if she could write three novels in a year, and then she wondered if she could even write one. She always wanted to do so, but all of her energy had gone into making tenure. This very situation, stuck in a tornado, would not be a terrible story, she thought. Unfortunately, she knew there was something missing.

Professor Schraeder returned after a few minutes and said things had improved. He said he wanted to return home because he wanted to prepare his dinner. Professor Williams did not believe him and went outside to check his findings. She exited the door that led to the center of campus and found the opposite of what Professor Schraeder had described. The sky looked like an enormous wedding cake that had fallen off the table. It had thick clouds the size of mountains with sharp textures similar to the swirls from a frosting gun, and they ran for miles above the bars, crops, and silos of Baxter County. The air was warm, but a cold breeze made Professor Williams shiver. She focused carefully on one of the spirals and realized it was slowly moving toward campus. A tail was forming a few miles behind, and it began to creep downward toward Earth like a secret weapon deployed by an alien race. She figured she had a few minutes before it would arrive, so Professor Williams rushed to catch up with Professor Schraeder.

She swiftly moved past the social sciences building and the coin fountain, but she did not find her colleague. She decided to change direction and headed toward the science building and its surrounding duck pond, but he was nowhere to be found. She took a short break next to the sitting statue of Robert Frost, and the two of them looked across the water.

"Maybe he's faster than I thought," she said. "Or maybe he decided to take the highway."

Professor Williams accelerated through the empty campus. A cold wind hit her face, and it dried the beads of sweat across her hairline. She then jumped a hedgerow of prairie grass and cow tails, landed on the highway pavement, and surprised a different man who was walking in her direction. She did not realize it was a priest until she saw his white collar. He stopped in front of Professor Williams and stared at her like she was a ghost—like he couldn't believe she was truly there—but she figured the storm had made everyone a little crazy.

She looked down the highway and caught the image of a tall man who was reading a book as he walked. Then she looked above him and noticed the clouds had changed direction and were now approaching the highway. Professor Williams yelled to Professor Schraeder to take cover in the ditch, but the power of the wind carried her voice in the opposite direction. She began to run toward him, but the wind picked up, and she could barely progress against its force. The tornado quickly approached Professor

Schraeder, and she closed her eyes before he disappeared inside the circulating movement of air, dust, and debris.

Professor Williams turned around, jumped the ditch of cattails and prairie grass, and continued moving until she was inside the McCutcheon Center for Sciences and Research. The front entrance featured an enormous window with thick glass through which students could observe the duck pond, the statue of Robert Frost, and a sun dial that had been donated by a wealthy alumnus. Professor Williams looked at the sundial through the window as she sucked air back into her lungs. The installment was anchored in a bank of cement, but the dial was not, and she watched the thick piece of iron spin like a toy.

A projectile interrupted her gaze. It was a bocci ball, likely from one of the student residences, and it seemed like it had been fired from a cannon. However, it did not penetrate the window. Instead, it became enshrined in one of the thick glass blocks, which were now adorned with fractures that ran from one end of the entrance to the other.

Suddenly Professor Williams felt a hand on her shoulder, but she continued to stare at the ball. Then the hand shook her body back and forth. She didn't realize she was in shock until she saw the concerned face of a young man behind her.

"Professor Williams. Are you okay?"

The hand belonged to Max Simmons, a student of Professor McKendrick. Max was tall and lanky, but he had the maturity of a much older man. Professor McKendrick had told Professor Williams that Max had a promising career as a physicist ahead of him.

"It's okay, Max. I was just startled."

"We need to get out of here."

"Where should we go? I don't know this building."

"Follow me."

Despite his heavy backpack, Max moved swiftly through a maze of hallways and short stairwells that turned at sharp right angles around classrooms and laboratories. Max moved confidently through the labyrinth, and she had trouble keeping pace. The shock from the previous events had not yet worn off, and she soon had no idea where the young man was taking her.

"We aren't safe until we're in the foundation," he said as he disappeared behind a door.

Behind Max she found the emergency stairwell that connected the floors of the building. The sound from the storm echoed through the room, but she could faintly make out Max's footsteps as he descended.

"Hurry up," he yelled from a few floors below.

The ground in the stairwell started to shake, and she had to move carefully down each step. She soon reached the bottom, and Max was standing next to a door with a look of frustration.

"It's locked," he said.

"So, what do we do?"

"This should be fine. We should be below the ground level by now."

"Where are we, exactly?"

"I don't know. We're probably on a garage floor. I bet that door leads to a supply room."

"I thought it was a bomb shelter."

"I guess they're not worried about that anymore."

Professor Williams sighed and rested her body against the wall. Max did the same, except he slowly slid into a sit.

"You might as well get comfortable. I think we'll be here for a while," he said as he rummaged through his backpack.

Professor Williams slid to the floor and caught her breath.

"Tell me something. How did you know my name?"

"You're Professor McKendrick's student. He told me a lot about you."

"Really?"

"Yeah, he seemed to think highly of you."

"What do you mean, *seemed*? Like, he doesn't think highly of me anymore?"

"No, that's not what I meant. It's that we don't really talk like we used to."

"I see. Yeah, he mentioned that things weren't going well."

"Wait . . . You mean, he talked to you about me?"

"Yeah, just every now and then."

"I see."

"Well, he and I are not really getting along right now, either," Max said.

"Why is that?"

"He thinks I stole something from him, but I didn't. Well, I did, but I didn't steal it. He and I have been working on a formula for a long time. It's a theory of time and, well, how you can *bend it* if you know certain things."

"What do you mean bend it?"

"Well, you can actually reverse time, but it only works in very specific situations. In fact, it only works once. Right now, everything is very preliminary. I, well, we haven't figured out a stable way of doing it."

Soon Max started looking through his bag. Professor Williams thought he was going to remove a notebook but instead produced a pipe and a lighter.

"Is this really the time for that?" she asked.

"You can turn me in if you want, but I have really bad anxiety. The tornado and, well, talking about my research, makes me need my medicine."

Professor Williams had never smoked marijuana, but no one had ever offered it to her, either. She knew most of the history and geology professors smoked, and they were as good as any faculty at the college.

Max lit the end, inhaled gently, and then released the plume in the opposite direction of Professor Williams.

"You see, we had been working for some time on a theorem related to the shape of the universe. Professor McKendrick had helped me put together a description of what I was seeing, but there was a missing piece. He told me to read a few articles, but none of them worked. Then one day I came across something strange in Professor McKendrick's office. I was helping him organize some papers for storage, and I found a piece of a document that I wasn't supposed to see.

"The paper had some strange language on it. Professor McKendrick said it might be Chinese, but it wasn't. The characters looked like hieroglyphics, and the more I studied them, the more I started to think they were coordinates or directions for a space ship."

Max lit the pipe again and offered it to her. She shrugged, took a small inhale, and began to cough. He asked if she was alright, and she said she was fine. He offered her more, but she declined. She took a deep breath and started to feel more relaxed.

"A space ship?"

"I know this sounds crazy... but listen. The whole thing became something of an obsession, but Professor McKendrick thought my efforts were misplaced. He even told me it was a hoax, just some crazy farmer with no idea about anything. I asked him why he kept a copy, but he didn't give me a good answer. He wanted me to keep going in the same direction, but I wanted to try something new. For some reason, I knew the missing piece to my theory was somewhere in the language, and, well, it was."

"What do you mean, *it was*?"

"I cracked it. I figured out the language."

"You deciphered an alien script?"

"Well, it wasn't alien, *per say*. It was physics, but with different symbols."

Professor Williams raised her eyebrows again.

"So, what did you find?"

"It was designed around some type of key directional text. I didn't have access to it, but by working backwards I figured out its general structure. The directions led to a focal point, a landing zone or something like that. I followed my calculations one day, and it led to a location only a few miles from here. It's right on the Callahan Ranch."

"So, what are you saying, exactly?" Professor Williams asked.

"I think Baxter County is a point on a grid that helps navigate travel through space."

"Does Professor McKendrick know about this?"

"Yes. I told him everything. I even showed him the calculations, but he thinks I'm crazy. He told me to quit working on *this absurdity* and to get back to my *real work*.

"The problem is that he started copying my work. One day the door to his office was open, so I walked in, and I noticed a problem on his desk. He was applying my theorem, and it looked like he had a breakthrough. Anyway, he walked in while I was reading it, and he got very angry and told me to get the hell out.

"Since then we haven't talked, but I've kept working on the formula. I wanted to figure out if I could bend time, and it turns out I can. In fact, it's not that hard. It just takes access to the right information, which I have right here."

Max put out the pipe and removed a notebook from his backpack. He flipped through the pages, which were filled with formulas that looked like an alien language in its own right. He flipped to the back page, and there he had a short formula, something simple that reminded her of an early lesson in a physics textbook.

"I built a microchip with the formula, and I rigged it to a remote control. I removed all the buttons except rewind because I can only move time backward. You just stand near a place where you want to go back in time, press the button, and, well, that's it."

"That is the most incredible story I have ever heard, Max."

"It's not a story, Professor Williams. It's real, and it's right here."

Max removed a remote control from his backpack. It looked like something from a garage sale.

"There's limits, though. It'll only work once, and it will only take the person holding it back a few hours. I don't know how many exactly, but it can't be more than three hours and fifty-eight minutes. Again, if my calculations are correct."

"So, are you going to use it?"

"Honestly, I don't know. What single event could really necessitate time travel? I think I'm going to wait until I really need it."

"I think that's a good idea," Professor Williams said. "How old are you anyway?"

"Why do you ask?"

"I don't know. You talk like someone older than an undergrad."

"I am, but it doesn't really matter."

Professor Williams thought about the stories Professor Schraeder had told her and realized she had all the missing pieces for her novel. She would name it after herself and describe the politics and pettiness of the people in higher education. She was only missing one piece, but that could be easily remedied. She looked at Max, placed her hand on his leg, and asked for another hit. She released the plume and moved her lips toward Max, but the moment was interrupted by a voice with a light German accent.

"What are you two doing down there . . . and what is that smell?"

Professor Williams withdrew from Max, rubbed her eyes, and saw Professor Brugenheimer on the stairs. She was standing next to her husband, Professor Koch, who also worked in physics. Max apologized to Professor Williams, the professors on the stairs, and quickly exited with his head down. The married couple shook their heads at the woman with glossy eyes at the bottom of the stairwell. They said they would talk about all of this later with the committee, but for now, she had better go home. Soon Professor Brugenheimer and her husband vanished, and Professor Williams noticed Max had forgotten his backpack and his remote control.

Professor Williams studied the device. She thought about what had happened, and then she thought about Professor Schraeder. She could push the button in this very place and maybe save herself, or she could push it on the highway, and maybe save her colleague. She wondered if she would remember what had happened during the time that would be lost, or bent, as Max kept putting it. She also wondered what would happen if it didn't work, and what the titles of her novels would have to be. She fixed her hair, released a deep sigh, and rested her head against the back wall.

Then she pushed the button.

"Chief" (Part II: The Cover Up)

The next morning Chief drank his coffee two stools from Nana at Peg's. The two men didn't speak, but they knew the other was there. The newspaper called for severe weather that afternoon, but neither seemed worried. The forecast was just an appetizer before the sports section, and they both had a lot of other things on their mind.

After breakfast Chief walked to City Hall to file a report. He noticed the sky had a color he used to see while driving through Oklahoma in springtime. During those days, he would spend hours in his rig watching the colors of the sky move from pink and red to violet and mulberry. For Chief, the morning pastels were the clearest indication that something big was on the horizon.

He entered the front door and was immediately approached by a man in a black suit. The individual was tall, bald, and wore a badge, but he didn't look like a cop. Chief noticed the man had an accent when he spoke, but he couldn't place it.

"Come with me," the man said.

Chief followed him down a hallway that led to a large door with a sign that read "The Office of The Mayor." The man gestured toward a couch and told Chief to wait there until his boss was ready to see him. Chief sat down and looked at the photos on the wall. The mayor had a picture with the governor, a few state senators, and even a man from New York who had run for president. Chief remembered the elections that year, but he didn't know who had won. He was in Baxter County, and everyone else was living somewhere far away.

Soon a door opened and a man in a blue suit approached him. Chief stood up and shook his hand, and the mayor introduced himself. He had a smile that seemed out of place, but he figured it was normal for a politician. It's probably a tool of the profession, he thought, like showing a badge or carrying a gun.

The mayor sat in a swivel chair behind an enormous oak desk covered with papers in several piles. Chief sat down on the other side and waited for him to speak. He knew what this was about, and he thought it best to stay quiet.

"Before we get to business, tell me about yourself."

Chief scratched his chest and smiled.

"I'm the sheriff," he said.

"Of course, I knew Sheriff Hardy for many years, and we had a great relationship, but I don't think you and I ever met formally. It has been on my list, but as you can see, I haven't been moving too quickly on anything. As sheriff, I'm sure you can relate."

Chief nodded.

"Anyway, Sheriff, what I wanted to ask you is what I can do to help you in your, umm, daily operations?"

Chief smiled.

"The truth is, Mayor, I think it's best to let everyone do their job. I'll leave you to the politics, and you let me handle the crime, and I think this whole county will be better off."

"Well, you see Sheriff . . ."

"Chief, just call me Chief."

"Well . . . Chief, unfortunately that's not how things work

around here. You see, my job is to oversee yours and that of many others. Now, the real issue here, of course, is the small event that took place last night. The state patrolman tells me you were acting recklessly in front of an armed perpetrator, and he pulled his gun to keep you both safe. I pulled the officer's file, and he had more complaints and citations in one year than most get in a career. Then I looked at yours, and frankly, I didn't see anything. No real citations, not a lot of arrests, and things have generally been pretty quiet around here since you took over.

"In most situations, Mr. Chief, I would say this is a pretty easy scenario, but that kid isn't just anyone; he's Senator Lang's nephew. Now, you may not know this, but I also have some ambitions that run beyond this fart of a town, and there is an election coming up. There's been a lot in the papers lately about cops and shootings, and frankly, it's better to keep all those things quiet. Long story short, all I need from you is a signature. Sign the report that the officer wrote up, and you and I won't have to see each other again until next year's Christmas Gala."

The mayor took a manila envelope from the top of a stack and removed a pen from his breast pocket.

"One signature, and I'll see you at the gala," he said with a smile.

The mayor extended a pen toward Chief.

"That's not necessary," Chief said. "I got one."

"Oh, that's even better," the mayor said. "I just thought you would enjoy using someone else's ink for a change. But anyway, now that we have that settled, let's talk about what I can do for . . ."

"You know where I got this pen?" Chief asked.

The mayor's grin began to fade.

"You see, this isn't my pen. It belongs to someone else. I'd say he gave it to me, but that'd be a lie. I actually stole it from a man. No kidding, I pulled it right off his dead body. You see, I got a report saying Hank Ford was brandishing a weapon at cars, but when I found him, the old man didn't have a knife or a gun. The whole thing could've been resolved last night, but a bad cop did a bad job. So now Hank isn't waking up at home. He's lying on a cold slab at the morgue, and frankly, I'm not okay with that.

"Now, Mr. Mayor, you've done a lot of talking, and I agree things would be easier if I just signed that piece of paper, but I wouldn't be doing my job, and you wouldn't be doing yours either. I'm sending in my report this afternoon, and if that costs me my job, well, that's fine. But me and Hank won't be the only individuals going down for it."

The wrinkles on the mayor's face grew hard.

"Unfortunately, that's where you're wrong, Sheriff. I know you're new here, but that's just not how things work. I'm going to give you some more time to think about this whole situation. In the meantime, you may want to think about what happens to unemployed cops with a note in their file."

The mayor stood up, shook Chief's hand, and then handed him a manila envelope with the report inside.

"In case you change your mind," he said. "I highlighted the place where the signature goes."

The door to the hallway opened as Chief approached it. The same man who met him at the front entrance was holding the door.

"Let's hope we do not have to talk again," he said with the accent that was hard to place.

* * *

Chief walked back to the station. He opened his office, threw the envelope on his desk, and then looked through the morning crime reports. At the top of the stack was a hit and run, but Chief couldn't focus. His mind returned to Officer Lang, Hank, and the mayor. Chief put the crime report away, took out a couple pieces of paper and a pencil, and started writing. He started with his name, the date, and his badge number. Then he started writing in paragraphs. When he was finished, he reread the whole letter out loud to himself. He added and cut sentences, changed words, and even found a few spelling errors.

Then he read it again, thought it was good enough, and rewrote the document in blue ink. He folded the pieces of paper, stuck them in a letter, and addressed it to *The Baxter Herald*. He licked the envelope shut, took a deep breath, and returned to the hit and run. A witness saw a blue truck collide with a green sedan around eleven o'clock the previous night. The driver of the sedan was taken to the hospital, and the blue truck drove off. A witness said the vehicle had just left Al's, and it was swerving until it collided with the sedan. Chief folded the report twice, put it in his pocket, and then went to talk to Al.

On his way to the bar Chief noticed the sky had in fact turned purple, and the puffy outlines of the clouds blended together like soggy mashed potatoes. He knew the rain would start soon, and then the hail, and then the winds. The air temperature also didn't seem right, which made Chief wonder if he should head back to the station before things got worse.

A crowd of people were leaving Al's as Chief entered. He asked if everyone was okay to drive, and they said what everyone says when they leave a bar.

"Just had a couple."

Chief then looked at a man who had more than a couple. He had a shaky hand and a bandage over his forehead. His name was Milliken, and Sheriff Hardy had arrested him for suspected kidnapping and murder. Everyone in town knew he killed his son, but the sheriff at that time didn't have the evidence to make it stick. Chief sat down next to Milliken, but he just ignored the sheriff. He didn't care for anyone wearing a badge, and so he just stared at himself in the bottles behind the counter.

Al finished cleaning a beer mug and then asked Chief what he needed.

"I'm looking for a truck," he said. "A blue one. Whoever was driving it was here last night, and he might've killed someone on his way out."

Al shook his head and pointed to Milliken.

"That's probably your guy," he said.

Chief ordered a couple of coffees. He said it was time to sober up, and that they needed to talk at the station.

Al removed the glass of whiskey in front of Milliken and said he could have it back when he was finished with Chief. He then poured two coffees and placed them in front of the two men. Chief took off his hat and ran his fingers through his white hair that ended in a ponytail, and then he took a long drink of coffee.

"These grinds are older than I am," he mumbled.

He waited for Milliken to take a drink and confirm his assessment, but he suddenly caught the image of a man on the sidewalk peering through the window.

"What the hell does he want?" Al asked himself out loud.

"Something with me," Chief said. "Do you know who he is?"

"He works for the mayor," Al whispered as the man approached the door. "But from what I hear he does a lot more than that. No idea where he's from, but he shows up uninvited a lot. There was an old dispute with some Indian land out by Callahan's farm not long ago. Someone on the reservation said he came by, made the shaman disappear, and the dispute suddenly went away."

Chief told Milliken to finish his coffee and go home. They still needed to talk, but this wasn't the time. The drunk nodded in agreement, but he didn't move from his barstool. Chief's attention was on the man at the window and the black town car that pulled up outside the bar.

The man approached Al and ordered two whiskeys. Chief rotated his stool in his direction and noticed a gun peek out from his belt. He stood several inches taller than the sheriff, and he was built like a water buffalo. He wiped his mouth and told Chief he had to come with him. He said the mayor wanted to give him a ride home before the weather got any worse, and they could discuss some things on the way. Chief knew he wasn't telling the truth, but he wasn't scared of anyone in a suit.

The men walked to a town car that was parked outside. A

driver hurriedly exited the driver's seat, walked to the door facing Chief, and invited him to have a seat. Then the sheriff felt a large hand on his shoulder.

"You'll need to leave that with me," the man said, pointing to Chief's gun.

Chief looked him in the eyes and saw the whole thing was a trap. He grabbed the man's arm to bring him down, but he was ready for the move and countered with a blow to the sheriff's stomach. Chief fell to his knees, and the man took his gun and threw him into the car.

* * *

The mayor waited patiently while Chief gasped for air in the seat next to him. The two were the only ones in the car with the driver as it moved out of town and toward an immense grey cloud. The mayor told Chief to relax and breathe, but the sheriff became agitated when he saw the cloud darkening the sky around them.

"Now it's my turn to be frank," the mayor said. "I'm going to give you one last chance to sign this piece of paper. Otherwise, this car is just going to keep driving until we arrive at a place outside of town. There, we'll meet with my associate, and he's not as nice as I am. But all that can be avoided if you just sign this piece of paper. Then we'll drop you off at home, and we can go our separate ways."

"You and your goons picked a bad time for an execution," Chief said. "I drove my old rig through the Midwest for years, and I've seen a lot of clouds like that one. This road might as well be leading to the end of the earth. If we keep driving straight, you, me, and that driver are all going to be drinking with Dorothy tonight."

The mayor looked through the windshield at the front of the car and became aware of the danger for the first time. He told the driver to stop the vehicle, and he stuck his head out the window.

"What do you think?" he said to the driver.

"I've been nervous since we got on this highway, but orders are orders."

"Do you hear that in the distance?" Chief asked. "Those sirens aren't a test, and that funnel is coming our way."

The mayor yelled to turn the car around as the twister formed above them.

"There's a storm drain coming out of a hill about a quarter mile back," Chief said. "We could probably fit inside it. That's our only chance."

The driver started the engine and accelerated into a U-turn that almost took the car into a cornfield. He hit the gas, and the vehicle lunged in the opposite direction of the twister.

"It should be coming up on the left," Chief yelled to the driver. "We only have a minute or so. You can't outrun a tornado."

Chief watched the cloud become thicker by the second. Then his eyes returned to the earth, and he saw the drain coming up on the left. He yelled to stop the car and told everyone to get out, but nobody did. The mayor was too scared to move, and the driver remained in his seat. Chief grabbed the politician by the collar of his sports jacket, dragged his body out of the car, and dropped him at the opening. The space was wide enough for both of them, but they had to lower their heads and crouch in order to move deeper inside the space.

A collection of rainwater, chemical runoff, and sewage immediately stained their pants and seeped through their shoes. The men sat at the edge of the dark storm drain, and they curled their bodies to avoid the small stream of waste water running below them.

"Where's the driver?" Chief asked.

"He's still in the car."

"Why the hell is he still in the car?"

"He lives at Sunny Side."

"He doesn't really think..."

"Yeah, he probably does."

The mayor grabbed Chief's arm.

"It's his own decision."

Both men looked out the tunnel. The wind screamed as

it passed the metal tube, and it fired rocks and other sediment against the black sedan.

"It's too late to help you now, hombre" Chief mumbled to himself.

The men inched closer to the opening as the air became colder. The wind changed from a single whistle to a high-pitched scream, and the sky became as dark as early evening. The car began to buckle from the pressure of the moving air, and it slowly lifted from the pavement. The window rolled down as the vehicle ascended, and the two men saw the driver wave goodbye as he disappeared into the enormous feather duster that had fallen from the sky.

The tornado disappeared once it had taken the car and the driver, but the wind and debris continued to circle. The men looked at each other and shrugged.

"I guess he'll be the one drinking with Dorothy."

The two sat in silence as hail began to fall. The first bits had the diameter of dimes, but they were followed by larger chunks the size of nickels and quarters. The ice bristled the grass, which had regained its color after the thaw, and the larger pieces exploded against the asphalt with the sound of a cracking rifle. The hail came in waves that intensified and slowed at the discretion of the changing winds, and it made Chief wonder what would have happened if they hadn't escaped the car in time.

The mayor, however, seemed disinterested in the storm and instead removed a pen from his sports coat. Chief recognized it immediately, but he didn't say anything. He just watched as the mayor unscrewed the head and collapsed it into two pieces. Then he took his thumb and index finger and popped out the small cylinder that kept the ink cartridge in place. He laid the pieces on the surface where they were seated, but he kept one of the small tubes from the bottom half of the pen in his right hand.

"You see, Chief, when you are in a situation like this one it doesn't matter what you do. It only matters who knows."

The mayor paused and then removed something from his

breast pocket. It was a small baggie, like something used for buying assorted beads, but it contained a white powder. The mayor tapped the baggie a few times until the substance covered his thumb knuckle and then used the pen to deliver the substance into his nose. Chief saw everything from the corner of his eye, but he decided to ignore it for now. The storm had moved through quickly, and it looked like they could leave the drain.

"The storm is settling," the mayor said.

Chief's fists were clenched when he exited the tube. He took a deep breath, and his fingers began to loosen.

"This isn't the time," he mumbled to himself.

Chief focused on a pile of trash that ran from the sewer to the road. The drain prevented Thompson Creek from flooding, and years before Chief arrived a weather pattern came through that brought rain showers that lasted for days. The banks of the creek overflowed, and the emergency sewer pipes saved the county from a biblical disaster. Nobody had inspected the drains or removed the garbage that had run this far outside of town, which is why beer cans, park benches, and even a busted shopping cart now ran from the sewer to the road.

Chief sighed at the landfill underneath his feet and then looked toward town. The twister was reforming above Main Street, and it seemed larger than the one they had just survived. Chief walked to the middle of the highway to get a better look, and he got a perfect view of the tornado as it descended toward Al's. Roofs began to detach from homes and businesses, but Chief fixated on the destruction of the powerlines. A transformer had burst, which sent a wall of fire down the power grid and a storm of orange, red, and yellow flashes onto Main Street. Chief hoped everyone in town had gotten to shelter in time, but he could still see small black dots looking for cover in the seconds before it arrived.

Chief looked back at the ground and noticed something out of place. There was a piece of metal a few inches across that did not resemble the other bits of waste on the grass. It looked like something from a science fiction movie because the metal was thin, translucent, and had three small, rock-like attachments protruding from one of its ends. He removed the object from the dirt, held it between his thumb and index finger, and observed a curvature at the center that could have only been made by a machine. Chief used his shirt to wipe the metal clean and realized the piece had been bent down the middle. He tried to unfold the metal, but it broke in half, and one of the small attachments fell to the ground. Chief picked it up, spit in his hand, and used the saliva to clean the dirt and sediment that had caked around the object. He then wiped it clean with his shirt and discovered it was an artificial molar. Chief began digging through the grass and dirt when the mayor interrupted him.

"What're you doing there, Chief?"

"Looking for something."

"Can I help?"

"Probably not."

"Are you sure?"

Chief had a hunch, and if he was right, it would put an end to a mystery that had bugged Sheriff Hardy for years.

"It's probably best you start walking to town," Chief said.

"Are you insane? It looks like aliens invaded. The whole place is on fire."

"Sounds like they need their mayor more than ever."

The mayor didn't respond. He just sat on a rock and took out his pen and baggie.

Moon Cheese

The tornado sirens went off as I opened the letter. Beat reporters like me don't get good news through the mail, and when I saw it was from the sheriff, I knew it was probably trouble. The lawmen that come through here don't usually have time for reporters, and when they need us, they think it's their job to write the story. People in this town have some strange ways of understanding the world, and it's my job to find the truth. The letter had a lot of conventions you might see in a cowboy movie or a detective story: senator's nephew, fictitious police report, innocent man dead on the asphalt. But I had reasons to think it wasn't a hoax. First, it was written by hand. If someone wanted to tell a lie or start a false rumor, they wouldn't expose their handwriting. Second, the spelling was atrocious, which made me think it was written quickly, perhaps by a desperate person who felt a lot of pressure to get the story out. There was also the timing. The letter arrived the same day it was sent, which isn't unusual in small places like these, but it was written only a few hours before a tornado was about to strike. The sheriff obviously felt there was no time to waste; he had to get the story out immediately. Maybe someone wanted him dead or maybe he was just worried about his good name. It's the letter every reporter hopes crosses their desk, and the story that could get me out of this cow town.

A second communication arrived in a shoe box a few days later. It contained a letter inside that explained the contents of two baggies, both of which contained a single tooth. The letter explained that Al, the barman, found the content of the first baggie in Milliken's backyard, and that Chief found the contents of the second baggie beneath a sewer drain on the outskirts of town. The letter said there were a lot more back at the station, but he wasn't sure what was going to happen. He said he wanted to be careful; he didn't want the teeth to fall into the wrong hands. Chief also said these were the most important pieces of a puzzle he didn't have time to solve. I didn't know what he meant right then, and I didn't know why he sent them to me, but I figured it had to do with that boy who disappeared a couple of years ago, and maybe the old man the patrolman shot on the side of the road.

I remember meeting the sheriff the day he swore into the position. It was a snowy afternoon in January, right after the new year, and there were only a handful of people in attendance. The weather reports were calling for a mild day, but a blizzard formed without warning and dumped thick sheets of snow on our hats and shoulders. The weather kept the mayor and most of the town council from attending, but the new lawman said that wasn't important to him. He said he did his best work when politicians did their jobs and left him to do his. He also said he was proud to work again in law enforcement, that it was an honor to serve the people of Baxter County, and that everyone in town didn't need to call him "Sheriff."

"Call me Chief," he said.

During our interview, he said a good sheriff is like a good sheep dog. You need to keep your eye on things, keep peace, and a low growl goes a lot further than a bark or a bite. I liked his style, but I wondered if it was too folksy. There were some tough guys in this town, and a lot of them didn't care for the law. One of the worst was named El Diablo. His real name was Nana Lightfoot, and rumor had it he was fleeing assault and murder charges in more than a few states. He didn't get along with Sheriff Hardy, and he even broke the lawman's nose when he cuffed him after a bar fight. Nana did some time for that one, and some more time for cracking skulls at another bar a town or two over. El Diablo liked to carry a gun on him, but he never took it out. I interviewed a guy at the hospital who got drunk and said something to Nana. It looked like the poor bastard had been shot in the face, but he assured me El Diablo only used his hands.

"He's possessed by the devil, but he's got an old spirit," the man said. "The gun is only there for the guys who don't play fair."

I made three calls that afternoon. I dialed the sheriff's office, the mayor's office, and the treasurer's office. A friend of mine works for the mayor, and she answered after the first ring. I met Janet the first time I tried to schedule an interview with her boss. I was new to *The Baxter Herald*, and I made all my appointments face to face. It turned out we both had graduated from the community college in town. She knew all the dirt in City Hall, but she told me she couldn't give too much detail. However, that rule didn't extend to confirming rumors, and we negotiated a system where I asked her questions, and she coughed if they were true.

"Janet, it's me," I said.

"You know a tornado is about to touch down outside?"

"There's a storm in the newsroom right now, too," I lied. "I just got a letter, and it sounds like something big went down last night. What do you know about it?"

"You know I can't talk to you about that stuff."

"This isn't a robbery. This is a murder, and the line leads back to some pretty big fish."

"I'm sorry, but I just can't."

"Well, a cop shot someone last night on the road."

I paused for a moment, and Janet coughed lightly.

"And it sounds like the sheriff was involved."

Janet coughed again, this time a bit stronger.

"And the guy who fired wasn't the sheriff but a state patrolman, someone related to the senator."

Janet groaned, which confused me. I stayed on the phone in silence and decided I'd say the same sentence again.

This time she coughed.

"I'd love to help you more," Janet said. "But the sirens are getting louder, and I just looked out the window . . . "

"Fine, just one last thing. There's a guy around here. You know who I'm talking about. The one who took care of things when the pushback came about the land deal on the reservation. He only shows up when The Mayor gets into trouble, and I saw him this morning leaving Peg's. I think he was looking for someone, and my guess is that person is going to disappear."

Janet coughed.

"I'm sorry, but I gotta go. There's a goddamn . . . "

The call dropped. I hung up my end of the receiver and returned it to my ear, but there was no sound. The phone lines were down.

Soon my door blew open, and the editor walked in.

"What the hell are you still doing here?" he yelled. "The biggest story this decade is coming down Main Street, and you're in here on your phone."

"I just got a letter, Luis. This is bigger than a twister. Something bad went down last night. Something big. And I think this goes all the way to the top. Sit down and give me a light."

I pushed a pack of cigarettes in his direction.

"You got two minutes," he said.

I waited until we took our first drag. Luis was clearly on edge, and he needed a second to calm his nerves.

"There's a guy I've heard a lot about since I moved here. Those who know him call him The Russian, but others think he's something else, like a ghost or something. Anyway, he's from out west, somewhere near Clarksdale, a shit town with an ore mine that closed years ago. The town had a community of Polish, Russians, and Bosnians who worked down there, but they had to close after the mine collapsed. I talked to a reporter out there who covered the story. He said The Russian was the only one to make it out alive. Everyone in town assumed God had saved him, but the reporter had a different idea. There was a connection between The Russian and some politicians in the area, ones who didn't like the mayor from that town. The journalist said The Russian sabotaged the mine so the town would shut down, and the mayor would have to go elsewhere. Well, it worked, and now The Russian is working in Baxter County."

"What does he have to do with a police shooting?"

"Chief wrote down the name of the patrolman who allegedly shot Hank Berry on the side of the road. The patrolman said Hank was armed, but Chief said he wasn't, and the patrolman said he was threatening the officers, which Chief also said wasn't true. The problem is that the patrolman, Curtis Lang, is the son of Perry Lang, our honorable senator. It seems to me The Russian is working for the mayor, and his job is to make the problem go away."

"What's the problem, exactly?"

"In some ways it's the shooting, but the real problem is Chief."

* * *

There were no dental records for Robert Milliken in Hooper. It's possible the boy never went to the dentist, and if he did, his mom took him somewhere outside the county. It wasn't easy to contact her, and when I did, she didn't want to talk. She said her son was gone, and no dentist was going to bring him back. I tried to explain the situation, but she wasn't listening. She said it was personal and none of my business. I couldn't deny she was right, but this was about more than her. She and her new husband stopped answering my calls after a few weeks, and I decided to show up unexpected. *She threatened to shoot me when she answered the door, but I told her she needed to see what I had. I held out the plastic bag with the tooth discovered in Milliken's backyard. She looked hesitant at first, but she eventually let me in. I talked for several minutes about what I knew, but she wasn't listening. She was busy inspecting the tooth, and after a few seconds she said it wasn't from her son. She said it didn't even seem human.*

"Maybe a deer or something."

Then I removed the other plastic baggie, which contained one of the teeth Chief found in the sewer. She rubbed it carefully with her right thumb and index finger and used her other hand as a bowl in case it fell. Soon she dropped the tooth into her left hand, closed it, and breathed deeply.

"Robert never went to a dentist," she said. "But I can tell you as a mother who has never been more certain of anything in her life that this tooth belongs to my son."

* * *

I handed Luis another cigarette. He rested it on his lip, lit it, and I followed him. We walked out the back door that opened to an alleyway behind a Mexican Restaurant known for its enchiladas. Luis lit my smoke, and we watched the clouds do things I'd never seen before.

"This is going to be a lot bigger than usual," he said. "This might be bigger than anything that's ever blown through this shithole of a town."

I lit another cigarette and exhaled as the wall cloud darkened the earth. The eclipse was total by the time I finished my cigarette, and I looked over at my editor. He released a puff of smoke that matched the feathery wisps that danced across the black hole above us.

"Severe weather always did funny things to me," Luis said. "I used to stare for hours at the spring clouds when I was growing up in Kansas. My neighbor was a cop, and she used to come out and yell at me to get inside. She told me I had a death drive, which I didn't understand then, but I don't think it's that. There's just something compelling about the sky, and so much you miss if you aren't paying attention."

Luis would do this from time to time. He'd close his eyes, imagine he's somewhere else, and talk about things that don't make sense. People who live here as long as Luis go a little crazy. Some of them move to the Sunny Side trailer park and start believing stuff about space ships. Others head to St. Michael's and start talking about Jesus. People like me read books and stick to the facts, although it's hard around here. Sometimes the fictions are the only stories that seem plausible.

"We got a few minutes until this thing touches down. Grab the camera. Let's take a few pictures for the front page."

We set up the camera under the gazebo in the town square. From there we could see all the local businesses and buildings: Al's, Peg's, Señor Enchiladas, City Hall, the medical center, and the surrounding neighborhood. We also had a clear view of the funnel as it formed in the distance. I stuck my face in the camera and started shooting the weather, the empty streets, and the people nailing boards across their doors and windows. Suddenly I saw something out of place, and I looked at Luis, who was already looking back at me.

"Do you see that, too?" I asked.

"Yup."

"What's the mayor's car doing outside Al's in the middle of a storm?"

"I can't say I have any idea," Luis said.

"Maybe I should take a few pictures."

* * *

I didn't think the worm child's mother was lying, but I wanted a second opinion about the teeth. I visited the town's only dentist, Doc Smiley, who was known for being old fashioned and a little mad. I told him it would only take a second, but he insisted I set up an appointment. He sat me in a reclined dental chair, and I showed him what I had. I removed the tooth from outside the storm drain, and he told me it looked like something from an adolescent. Then I pulled out the other tooth, the one from Milliken's backyard. He looked at it, furled his brow, and then gave me a serious look.

"Where'd you find this?" he asked.

I told him it was part of an investigation, but I didn't reveal any more details. He moaned something to himself, removed his glasses, and told me to follow him.

We walked down a hallway that turned at sharp angles after every few feet, and then we descended a poorly lit stairwell to a door with a name tag that read "Bob Smiley." The dentist removed a key from his lab coat, opened the door, and flipped a switch that turned on a large lamp in the shape of a tooth. The office contained a makeshift dental laboratory filled with decommissioned instruments, drills, and a wall of prosthetic teeth. Doc Smiley closed the door behind me and sat at a desk with an enormous magnifying glass attached to an adjustable arm used to search for sores and ulcers. He put on a new pair of glasses lying on his desk and carefully studied the teeth from the two bags.

"This is very interesting," he said. "Very interesting."

I asked him what he was thinking, but he ignored me.

"Very, very interesting."

I stayed quiet until he finished his examination. He moved the magnifying glass away from his eyes, and it rested in a position directly in front of his mouth. The optic tripled the size of his lips and teeth, and he spoke with sighs between sentences.

"It happened a long time ago," he said. "I was with a friend of mine, Callahan, who was telling me stories about space ships and the like. He said the creatures stopped by after nightfall, and that he'd take me out by the railroad tracks and the cemetery to *see them. We were a few beers deep, and I told him they couldn't be worse than the people on this planet. He knew every inch of the property and effortlessly avoided rocks, weeds, and cow pies, but I wasn't so lucky. I was scraping shit off my boot when he told me to look up, and there I saw it.*

At that point, the dentist removed a pack of cigarettes from his desk. He asked me if I smoked, and I told him I didn't. He shrugged, lit a cigarette, and told me I was full of shit.

"I bet you're one of those patients who can't say three truths in a row," he said. "Your teeth are the color of a brown squirrel."

His cigarette looked enormous behind the magnifying glass, which also magnified his tongue as he talked.

"Anyway, I looked up, saw the craft, and the next thing I knew I was lying in a cemetery. I had nightmares for weeks, and they were vivid. I could see their small, grey bodies, and the jagged teeth they use to tear up livestock. I know all this sounds crazy, but I can tell you without a doubt in my mind that this tooth, the one from the backyard, is from a grey.

"And the other one, the tooth from the sewer?" I asked.

"Looks like a kid's tooth."

* * *

We took photos as The Russian punched Chief in the stomach and stuck him in the mayor's town car. Then we watched The Russian as he got into a truck and drove in a different direction. Luis said the company van was parked outside, that he had the keys, and that we could catch up once we were on the highway. I pointed to the clouds, and he agreed it was a stupid idea.

"Let me handle the driving. I need you to take pictures."

The van was large, white, and had *The Baxter Herald* printed on the sliding doors. There were no other cars on the road, so we ignored the stop signs and drove as fast as the van allowed. I asked Luis if he had ever followed a car before, and he smiled.

"You mean you've never tailed a suspect?" he laughed.

"An ex-lover or two," I said. "But nobody carrying a gun."

"You know I was a private investigator before I became a journalist?" he said. "I had a niche for catching bad husbands, bad nannies, and bad employees. You get a corrupted view of the world when you spend all day videotaping these people, but the work was fun, and I was good at it. In reality, the two jobs are pretty similar. It's just that one ends in court and the other ends on the front page."

He rested a cigarette on his lip, lit it, and kept driving.

"You know this place wasn't always like this. There was a time before the mayor and a time before the curse."

I paused before lighting my cigarette.

"Nobody's told you about the curse? It goes back to when they discovered oil on the reservation. The mayor and his goons buried the right people, and they got part of the land. The well exploded after about a month of drilling. It wasn't far from the Callahan Ranch and some old railroad tracks that hadn't been used for decades. It happened in the middle of the night, and it sent badly burned and mutilated bodies flying for miles. They never found all the victims. Some say the land swallowed them to make up for what they had taken. "Blood for oil," they say. Others say some nonsense about aliens and space crafts. Then the floods came. It rained here like it was the end of days, and it washed out the crops and put generations of farmers out of business. These twisters we've been having aren't surprising. They're just part of the curse, and if you ask me, it's a good idea to leave town before the twister arrives."

The funnel was now in full view, and it appeared to be running down the highway where The mayor's car was headed. It was several miles east of our location, and we wondered if they had turned around or taken cover. We were far enough away to be safe, but we knew that could change at any moment. The black truck soon turned off the highway and onto a county road. We kept driving straight, and I asked Luis if we should keep following him.

"If we turn onto that road he'll know we're on their tail. There are some binoculars in the back and a telescopic lens in the camera bag. We'll park behind the ravine where it's safe and watch him from there."

I put the binoculars to my eyes and watched The Russian lean against his vehicle. It looked like he was waiting for someone to arrive, and I imagined it was Chief and the mayor. There was a pistol sticking out from behind his jacket, and it wasn't hard to imagine a shovel in his truck. He seemed calm and didn't move much, like he was both present and absent at the same time. I wondered if he had done this before and if the miners knew what happened when their world collapsed around them.

"The people on the reservation think he's the devil, and it might be true, but I bet he'd die if the right person shot him."

* * *

Dr. Gutierrez had a degree from an Ivy League school behind his desk, and he moved a quarter over and under his fingers as he spoke. He had gel in his hair, a checkered shirt, a blue tie, and a tailored sports jacket. He was an anomaly in these parts, and I asked what he was doing in a place like Hooper.

"I specialize in bovine cancer," he said. "For me, this place is a gold mine."

"I came across some teeth while doing a story, and I'm curious to know what you make of them. I asked a few people, and all are pretty sure of what they are, but none of their stories seem right."

I handed over the baggie with the tooth from outside the sewer. Dr. Gutierrez looked at it and said it could be from a predatory animal, but it's probably human, likely from an adolescent male.

"I'm tempted to ask you how such a tooth came into your possession, but frankly, it might be better if I didn't."

I nodded and handed him a bag with the tooth from

Milliken's backyard.

"This is a lot more interesting," he said. "The grooves are curious, like something you'd find in an omnivore, but the shape isn't right. It could be a human with a strange form of tooth decay, an animal whose remains had been burned, or something that we simply haven't discovered yet."

I asked him what he thought such an undiscovered creature might look like, and he looked out the window and smiled.

"I guess that all depends on where you're from and what you believe."

"What do you mean?"

"A few culprits come to mind, but I have experiences that go way beyond science and medicine. You see, my family lived for generations in New Mexico, and I remember my grandmother would tell us stories about strange creatures—monsters for lack of a better word—and people with magical powers.

"Her favorite was the crying woman, La Llorona, whose children drowned in a river not far from our house. La Llorona was so sad that she killed herself shortly after, and since then, she patrolled the area after nightfall calling to her children. If she found us outside after bedtime, grandma would say, then La Llorona would put us in her bag and keep us for her own. At school, we talked among one another and learned that the same woman patrolled other neighborhoods too. Some of the kids said the whole thing was a hoax, and that we were silly for believing it, but other kids weren't so sure.

"I suppose I believed my grandma more than others because she was a curandera, a medicine woman. In that time and in that part of the country there weren't doctors, nurses, or prescriptions. If you were sick you came to our house and saw my grandmother. She knew all the plants with medicinal qualities and the prayers that accompanied them. She cured infections, sicknesses, and delivered hundreds of babies. She also knew a lot about animals and cures for their basic ailments. I wanted to become a veterinarian after she cured a dog that ate a bad

piece of chicken. She fed it a mixture of milk, rose roots, and a green plant that only grew during the first weeks of spring on the backside of the hills surrounding our property. For two weeks the animal became stronger, but the people who brought us the dog never returned. I named him Javier and cared for him until I was old enough to go to college, which was about the time the town changed. People stopped coming to see my grandma for medicine, and they started calling her a witch. I was already in the northeast when she fled with Javier.

"Nobody saw my grandmother or the dog again except for me. She appears sometimes when I'm alone at home. I'll sit down in my chair with a book, and suddenly I'll smell the lilac and lavender she would gather on the llano. She'll appear in a smoky form, sit at the chair in front of me, and we'll have conversations that seem to last for hours. I tell her how I have been, and she tells me how much she misses me and the family. Unfortunately, the last time we talked she didn't think she'd return. She said she'd have Javier follow me in case I ever got in trouble, and I know it's true because I see him from time to time. Back during the floods, I got a call to help birth a cow on the Callahan Ranch. I took a shortcut through a small park on the way home, but the bridge on the path was swaying from the wind and the rising waters.

"I decided it was best to go another way, but I noticed a kid moving toward the bridge. He was on his knees, and it looked like he was removing something from the ground. Unfortunately, it was hard to see from the heavy rain, and I couldn't tell if he was ignoring me or just couldn't hear my voice. I called out to him repeatedly, but he just kept moving toward the structure that was clearly going to collapse. I knew I had to do something, so I began to run toward him. I was only a few feet from the bridge when I suddenly felt a sharp pain in the back of my leg, and I fell to the ground.

"It felt like something had sunk its teeth into my ankle, and I felt blood when I rubbed my hand across the wound. When I finally got to my feet I saw Javier on the bridge, crouched like a *wolf ready to pounce. I couldn't tell if what I was experiencing was real, so I took another step toward the child, and the dog once again lowered, ready to attack. I looked at the boy, then at the dog, and I took a step back. I continued yelling at the boy, but he just kept walking toward the bridge. Javier disappeared when the middle of the structure gave in, and the boy fell into the rushing waters. I didn't tell anyone about it because I figured nobody would believe me, or worse, they'd think the New Mexican guy in town, me, may have thrown him in. Anyway, I'm certain if I hadn't seen that dog I would have gotten on that bridge and never made it to the other side.*

"To answer your question, maybe it's a ghost dog, a coyote-like creature that attacks livestock, or an enormous snake that lives near the river. All of these things are real according to my family, but that's probably not what you're looking for. So, tell me again, where'd you find it?

* * *

The Russian looked at his watch, got back into the truck, and drove to town. The twister had already moved through the town square, and we could see smoke from an exploded transformer and debris from barns, houses, and windmills. We drove slowly on the highway dodging pieces of roofing and drywall that had been taken to the sky. Luis said we were probably at the portal of the cyclone.

"Sometimes these storms suck up everything and kick it out within a small area of about a mile or two. Keep your eyes out, there might be all types of debris."

We passed a house that had been lifted off the ground and crushed in the air, a harvester wheel, dozens of garden gnomes, and a couple drunk farmers on the side of the road. They were loading a cow in the back of their truck, and for some reason it had a rosary around its neck.

"This place gets weirder every time I leave the office," Luis said.

The sky began to clear as the storm clouds dissipated across the prairie. We zig-zagged around a propane grill, three wooden stock crates, and a car door that led to a black town car. Luis stopped the van, and I knocked on the tinted window. Soon the glass lowered and a man with a driver's hat greeted us with hysterical laughter and an empty bottle of bourbon.

"I never saw this one coming," he laughed. "Just when I thought I had The Leader all figured out."

He continued speaking nonsense until Luis told him to be quiet for just a second.

"What are you doing out here, and where are the people you were driving?" he asked.

The driver chuckled at the question and then continued laughing for no apparent reason. Luis looked at me, and I shrugged. Then the man started to calm down.

"It was the damn twister," he said. "It took me way up there, waaaaaaay past the clouds, and across the other side. You see, The Leader had planned for all of this, but I wasn't expecting it today. What do the Christians always say? Be ready for the coming? Well, it was today, and it was right atop my car, and I sure as shit wasn't ready. Goddamn hilarious, all of it, if you ask me."

"What happened to Chief and the mayor?"

"Those two? Oh, they told me to stop outside a sewer drain a few miles from here. They ran out like a couple of idiots. They didn't realize what was happening. They thought it was just a tornado. Poor bastards had no idea what they were up against. You see, they didn't realize all of this was from The Leader."

"You must be from Sunny Side."

"That's right, but don't think I'm one of those lunatics out at the trailer park. I'm a lot more than that. You see, a lot of people just regurgitate things about The Leader they hear from other people. I actually got the book, the one written by The Leader, for the select few who know about its potential. Me and my buddy Hank Berry worked for a long time to get it into the Baxter County library, and then some librarian stole it and gave it to the town drunk. Anyway, I broke into their house and stole it back while they were at the Enchilada joint, and I found a few other things that caught my interest. The drunk, Milli-something, found a sign from The Leader—a rock that was caked in something very special."

The driver looked around him, signaled us to come closer, and whispered in our direction.

"The moon cheese," he said.

I looked at Luis, and he shrugged his shoulders.

"The what?"

"Moon cheese. You see, every couple of millennia The Leader sends a sign from the other side. The most recent was a rock that landed on some property out by the Callahan Ranch. It was covered with a substance filled with spores that grow over time. You see, the book gives clear indications that eventually the people of Earth will be wiped away and replaced with those of us who believe in The Leader. Anyway, the rock was sitting in the drunk's tornado shelter, and I took it home and stuck it in my trailer, along with the book. The moon cheese is going to keep growing, and eventually the creatures that come out will put an end to everyone and everything on this miserable planet."

"And what's going to happen to you?" I asked.

His grin disappeared.

"That's the tricky part. You see, the tornado was supposed to take us to the other side until things cooled down, and we could return to Earth. I thought that tornado was going to take me along, but apparently it wasn't in the plan. Instead, I'm here, back on Earth."

"So, I guess you should destroy the rock?" Luis asked.

"Maybe, but it's hard to say. Maybe it's a test of faith. Or maybe the whole damn thing is a hoax."

"This would be the best story ever written in *The Baxter Herald*," I whispered to Luis. "Too bad it's all bullshit."

"As far as your friends, well, the big one is probably dead.

When they have me drive people out to the corn fields that means they're going to meet up with another guy, a scary one. I usually drop them off, drive around for a little while, and when I come back, there's usually one less person in the car. I don't ask any questions though. That's not my job. I just get the mayor from A to B."

I looked at Luis, who shrugged his shoulders and said we should probably get back. We headed down the highway, turned into the town square, and headed back to *The Baxter Herald*. We were about to park when Luis pointed to a tree that had fallen through Al's, and I told him to stop the car because I wanted to take a picture. I got out, started walking toward the bar, and noticed the black truck we had been following. It was parked outside the bar, and was a little crooked, like it had stopped in a hurry. Suddenly I heard a gunshot, and then one or two more. I thought about turning around, but my legs kept moving toward the action. I swung open the main door, and I saw Chief, The Russian, and El Diablo standing near the bar. Nana didn't see me, and The Russian was bleeding on the ground. Chief, however, was staring directly at me. Soon he lifted his finger and pointed at me.

"That's her. She always protects me."

"Chief" (Part III: The Conclusion)

Chief used his hands to filter the dirt and search for anything that wasn't garbage or sediment. After a half hour, he had discovered a handful of teeth. The mayor asked what the teeth were from, and Chief told him they were from an animal. The mayor thought about asking him more questions, but he decided to change the subject. He asked Chief how he got to Baxter County.

"Family," Chief said. "My grandma and her family got put on the reservation near the Callahan Ranch when she was young. The land was too sandy for crops, and animals were scarce, so the men took jobs working the railroad. They worked day and night but were still dirt poor and had to come to town and beg for sugar and flour to survive. Grandma passed when I was young, and my mom disappeared around the time they found oil on the land. My cousins put me up after my accident. Now I help them the best I can. That's just what we do. We help each other when someone needs it."

"Who was your mom?" The mayor asked.

Chief looked at him with a gaze the mayor had never seen before. It was like he was a different person, someone a lot less predictable than the town sheriff.

"Well, it depends who you ask. If you were white, you called her a healer; if you were Mexican, she was a *curandera*, but everyone on the reservation, those who knew her, called her the shaman."

The mayor looked at the bones again and began to sweat through his shirt.

"There was a flood awhile back. I bet you remember it. The one that drowned the crops and filled the streets with garbage. That all happened after my mom disappeared. But I bet you don't know anything about that, Mayor. The whole damn thing was probably just a coincidence."

The mayor needed water, but he didn't have any. Instead, he gathered his fingers and took another sniff from his baggie.

"She keeps an eye on me from the other side. She protects me."

The mayor licked his finger and collected the last bit at the bottom.

The men walked in silence until they saw someone approaching from a dirt road that led to a few small farms and St. Michael's Church. The man's head was down, and he was praying the rosary in a loud voice as he walked. They could tell he was a priest because he was wearing black pants, a black button-up shirt, and a white collar. Chief and the mayor expected to hear Our Fathers, Hail Mary's, or a Glory Be as they got closer, but he was praying something different.

He was mumbling things about aliens, a church, and the end of days. Then he started speaking a language Chief couldn't understand. The man looked foreign, so maybe it was his native tongue, but something about it seemed off, like he was possessed by something he couldn't control. The mayor told him to slow down and explain what was going on, but the priest didn't respond. He walked and spoke in tongues until he disappeared.

Both men wondered if they had seen a ghost, but they kept the idea to themselves. The mayor figured it was a delusion from the powder in his baggie, and Chief had seen enough ghosts not to get too excited. Plus, Chief had been thinking about something else.

"You know, I realized something a little bit ago."

"What's that?" the mayor responded.

"Back in town when you picked me up. Nobody saw me get into the car except Al, who's a good friend of mine, and Milliken, the drunk."

The mayor didn't respond.

"It'd be different if someone had seen me, that's all," Chief said.

"What are you talking about?"

"When you work in law enforcement, you don't just think like a cop. You start thinking like a criminal, too."

The mayor stayed silent.

"You see, Mayor, nobody knows it yet, but you and I are ghosts."

The mayor's body heated up again and sweat now seeped through his sport coat.

"In a few days, someone will file a missing persons report, and I'll probably lead the search until the state boys take over. They'll have helicopters and hound dogs scanning every ditch and corn cob, and soon enough they'll find whatever is left of the car and maybe even your driver."

The mayor looked over at Chief.

"The mystery will bring a lot of attention to town, and there will probably be news cameras set up across City Hall for weeks. I'll probably give nightly updates on the search, but you and I both know that they'll never find anything."

Chief stopped walking and put his left hand on the mayor's shoulder to slow him to a stop.

"Maybe we should take a trip to my family's old land. There's a spot beside some old railroad tracks that you'd love. The land is tough, so tough it's hard to dig a grave, but there's a cemetery for people who used to lay the tracks. Nobody ever goes out there because everyone knows it's haunted. Yeah, it'd be a good spot for you, Mayor.

Chief squeezed the man's shoulder blades until he fell to his knees.

"The truth is, they'll quit looking for you after three weeks."

The mayor began to talk quickly. He said he could talk to someone about the report. He said he could make the whole thing go away. He said he didn't have to see their farm. He said the whole thing could go away tomorrow.

"And why should I believe you?"

"Because I'm giving you my word," the mayor said. "And my word is gold."

* * *

The sheriff returned to Al's the next day. It was only noon, but the bar was filled with familiar faces. A tree had fallen through the glass window facing the sidewalk, and the patrons were using the tree as a table.

"I wish we'd get these storms more often," Al said. "I've never seen so much business since the twister and that damn tree."

Chief took his hat off, nodded to the faces he recognized, and took a seat at the bar.

"Can I get you a beer, Sheriff?" the bartender asked.

"I don't drink," Chief said. "All I want is to find Milliken."

"He's probably at home sleeping off his hangover. He won't be sober enough to talk until this afternoon. Your best bet is to wait for him here. He usually rolls in around three or four. But in truth, Sheriff, there's something else you should know about. You see, Milliken stuck around last night, and he took shelter with us down in the basement. We got to talking, and he invited me over to his house. He got his usual drunk and passed out, and I noticed some things around his house that made me suspicious. Anyway,

I started rooting around his backyard and found something big. I think I cracked the case, Sheriff."

"What'd you find?"

"I'll show you."

Al disappeared into the back room.

Chief waited for Al to return and caught the movement of a large man outside the bar looking in. Al soon returned with a brown bag.

"Maybe we should go somewhere more private?" Chief whispered.

"Nobody here gives a damn," Al said. "The nice thing about drunks is they don't care about anything but their booze."

Al placed something in front of Chief, and he examined it closely. The sheriff mumbled something under his breath, and then Al handed him another.

"Where'd you find these?" Chief asked.

"In Milliken's yard, hidden beneath a brush pile."

"And I'm guessing you think this is his son's?" Chief said.

"That's right. Doesn't look like any coon bone I've ever seen."

"You're right," Chief said. "But I don't think these are human."

"They aren't?"

"I can't be sure, but they look like deer bones. Are there any teeth?"

"Yeah, a few."

"Put them in a bag, and I'll show them to a few people."

Suddenly their attention moved to a large man in a suit walking through the door. Once inside, he approached the bar and told Al he had to talk to his friend.

"The Sheriff and I are busy," Al said.

"Mr. Chief and I need to talk," he said.

"We're almost done here, and then you can talk to whoever you want. In the meantime, have a seat and I'll get you a drink."

"I'm afraid it's too late for that. Mr. Chief and I have a real problem."

His voice grew louder, his accent got stronger, and the

patrons started to leave. Bar fights weren't uncommon at Al's, and most knew it was best not to get caught in the middle.

Chief got to his feet and quickly remembered the man's size. He was younger, taller, and fitter than the sheriff. He also had Chief's gun.

"You shouldn't have dropped your weapon," the man laughed. "Now, let's go out back. There's a dumpster that's perfect for this type of reunion."

The Russian drew the sheriff's pistol and told the lawman to walk. Chief knew the place to make his move was at the door, but he also knew the man would be expecting it, and he'd have no problem spilling his brains across the back room. Instead, he grabbed a beer bottle and threw it at the man. He hoped it would distract him for just a second, but it didn't. Instead, the man pulled the trigger and shot Chief in the shoulder. The bullet went through his arm and exploded the mirror and a bottle of cheap whiskey.

"I thought you'd want to save your bartender friend some hassle," the man said. "But I guess you'd rather die here. That's fine with me."

"Just one second," Chief said. "At least let me look you in the eyes."

Chief rested his shoulders against the bar, got himself into position, and was ready to tell the man to fire. However, their attention was suddenly diverted to the bathroom door. El Diablo appeared, and he didn't hesitate. He fired three bullets, and the sheriff's assailant fell dead.

Suddenly Chief felt a cool breeze across his face. He thought he was dying, but he realized it was coming from the front door. He wasn't sure if he was dreaming, but he could make out the shadow of a woman.

"It's my mother," Chief said to Nana, who was crouched beside him.

El Diablo didn't know what he was talking about. All he saw was the new journalist in town, the blonde woman who was always taking pictures and asking people questions.

"You all right?" Nana asked.

"Just a scratch."

"Didn't see you at Peg's this morning. Let's clean you up and get some eggs."

Funeral Sandwiches

Father Nguyen's thoughts move to the rhythm of the rosary. Spoken aloud and in rhythm, the Hail Marys sound more like a chant than a prayer. He recites a Glory Be and returns to the tornado shelter, the church, and the cloud that hovers above him. There he feels safe because he can make a different decision.

This time I get to the door.

Everyone makes it out but me.

A child waves as I disappear into the sky.

Each word moves the story forward and then rewinds it. He makes the same decision and escapes with his life. He makes a different decision and disappears with everyone else. He makes a third decision, and everyone escapes but him. He cannot imagine a scenario in which everyone lives. He tries, but his mind won't allow it. A happy ending is incongruent. A sacrifice must be made. A savior must be born.

Professor Anderson looks at his friend beside him. The man

is tall, has long, dark hair, and his mind is elsewhere. The man imagines being back in his basement with a physics problem in front of him. The theorem does not work, and he wonders if it's nonsense. He rethinks the problem, but something is off. He has a feeling about it, though. He has read and reread the calculations, and they make sense, but something is missing. There is something he cannot explain. Then he thinks about Professor Williams and their time together. It was everything he wanted, but he was not happy. Maybe that would change over time. Maybe they're supposed to be together. Maybe true love isn't about true happiness.

He thinks about the strange language from Callahan Ranch. He thinks about the Chinese and the Irish. He thinks about the space ship and the old man. Perhaps the storm will bring more rain. It has been another year of drought.

Has there ever been a good year?

It's the Midwest.

We've been doing this since the wagons.

Chief stands behind Milliken. His arm is in a brace, and his shirt covers stitches and gauzes. He was going to see the doctor, but he left because the line was too long. He said other people needed the attention more than him. After getting some eggs, he decided to check out the trailer park. He walked across the area and didn't find a person, cat, or paint can. No families came looking, either.

He wonders where the people of Sunny Side went. He wonders if they were on to something, maybe they were right all along.

A boy stands next to his mother and follows the beads. He lost count, but he thinks they're on the seventh Hail Mary and the third decade. His eyes are closed, but he isn't thinking about God or the dead. He wonders about his cow and what would have happened if his father had not found him. He also thinks about the paper he found in the cemetery. He found a Chinese textbook at the library, and none of the characters looked right. Maybe it wasn't a human language, he thinks. Maybe it really was from a space ship.

Then he thinks about his grandpa. The old man spends all day looking at the clouds. He is at home and is probably thinking about the weather, or the aliens, or maybe his wife who passed to the other side. He looks to his right and sees Terrence Heckley and his grandma. His mom always said not to stare at Terrence. The boy tries not to, but he can't help it, and Terrence smiles and waves. The grandma tells Terrence to stop and then shoots the young boy a look, and he feels bad for staring.

Al sits in the front row thinking about the shovel, the dirt, and the bones. He wonders if there is more to this world than a bar in Baxter County. Then he thinks about his poems. He writes them when his wife is at the store. She comes home and reads every word. She likes the ones about nature and animals, but she doesn't understand the poems about time. They are long, difficult, and use words she has never seen before. She wonders where he learned certain words and how he imagined some of the ideas. Maybe he has friends and experiences that she doesn't know about, or maybe he reads books she's never found. When she reads his poems, she wonders if she really knows her husband, or if he's searching for something outside Baxter County.

The fields are the ocean.
The corn is my sea.
The buzzards are the pelicans.
Manure in the breeze.

All eyes in the church return to Father Nguyen as he reads the names of the churchgoers: Professor Schraeder, his dearest friend The Monsignor, Father Ellison, and more. Then he asks for a moment of silence. Those in attendance think about the people they knew. They go back to their previous thoughts, their concerns, and their beliefs. Many also wonder about death.

Maybe it is a myth; we all return to life.

Maybe it's angels and harps, fire, and brimstone.

Maybe it's our perception of nothing, the space two inches behind our heads.

A man in a black suit approaches the podium. He introduces himself as the mayor, but everyone knows who he is. He talks about the lives of the people lost, and how the town and the rest of the county will endure. Then he talks about God, Catholics and Protestants, the cross, and the promise of rain in the coming months. The people like the sound of the words, even though they don't know what they mean, and he would have received a boisterous applause if they weren't standing in the house of the Lord.

Father Nguyen thanks Pastor Thompson for letting them use their church, and he invites everyone to the cafeteria for sandwiches and coffee. In times like these, all Christians must come together.

Professor Williams watches from the back, but she isn't interested in the funeral or Professor McKendrick. She is here to say goodbye to Dr. Schraeder.

She got word that her colleagues in Modern Languages would recommend her for tenure. Professor Brugenheimer and her husband took leave for medical reasons, but they never explained why. Professor Jiménez said the two professors were different after the tornado. Some say they went on vacation. Some say they fell ill. Others say their memories had been completely erased.

Professor Anderson talks to Father Nguyen in the line for sandwiches.

"It was a very nice ceremony," Professor Anderson tells him.

Father Nguyen thanks him for the kind words and tells him it has been a difficult few days. Professor Anderson agrees and then focuses on the plate in front of him. The bottom half of his white bread is covered with two pieces of ham and a slice of American cheese. He spoons mayonnaise on the top half, smears it, and completes his funeral sandwich. He adds pasta salad that was donated by a parishioner, a handful of chips, and a cookie. Father Nguyen follows a similar course, but he opts for turkey and extra lettuce.

"So, what is your opinion of all this?" Father Nguyen asks Professor Anderson.

"All of what?"

"All of it, I suppose."

"Well, to be perfectly honest, I'm a man of science more than God."

Father Nguyen nods, but he doesn't seem convinced. He looks at the two piles of cold cuts and then asks him why it couldn't be both.

Professor Anderson has never considered a third option. It seems convenient but entirely impossible.

"You have to make a decision, evolution or divine intervention."

"Why can't God have created evolution?"

"The science doesn't support that."

"What about the universe?"

"What about it?"

"Why couldn't God have created the universe?"

Professor Anderson chuckles. It is a possibility, but one he can't take seriously. Not with what he knows about matter, the big bang, and the expanding universe.

"Because I know exactly when it started and how. I can prove it."

"How does one prove it?"

"Well, it requires a lot of calculations, things most people struggle to understand."

"Is there any faith involved?"

"What do you mean?"

"I mean is there any grey matter? Anything that has not yet been answered?"

"Well, of course."

"Tell me, Professor Anderson, what do you think exists at the edge of the universe?"

"Nothing."

"What is nothing?"

"It's nothing, the absence of matter."

"Perhaps that's where God lives."

"It's a nice idea, Father. I'll think about it."

Professor Anderson looks for Professor McKendrick, but he is talking to Professor Williams. Professor Anderson takes a bite of his sandwich and sees that Father Nguyen is looking at him.

"You know, I studied biology before I became a priest, and I never had trouble balancing it with my beliefs. I suppose I always thought religion preceded the sciences. Maybe it was because religion was the first class of the day, or maybe because I saw the sciences as a way of studying God. I thought if I could learn all of it, I would have a better understanding of how He thinks."

Professor Anderson nods as he finishes his sandwich. He looks to see if there is more bread, and then looks back at Father Nguyen. He thinks about telling the priest why God is an impossibility, but he decides this isn't the time for it.

"And you, Father. What do you make of all this?"

"Of science and God?"

"That and everything else."

"Well, when you read a lot of scripture you think a lot about parables."

"What do you mean?"

"Well, a parable is a short, didactic story that uses metaphors to teach larger lessons about the world, God, and our relationship with both."

"I see."

"What I mean to say is that everything that happened . . . it sounds more like a parable than reality. It's like The Lord is trying to make an example of us . . . like he wants to teach us something. And, to be frank, Professor Anderson, I don't know what to make of it. Noah knew to build an ark, and Mary knew to bear a child, but my task is not clear. In truth, I fear it was all an accident or that it is meaningless. Maybe I was supposed to die, but I didn't. What is a priest without a flock, a mission, or a God?"

Professor Anderson doesn't know what to say.

"A science professor?"

Father Nguyen chuckles and looks at his sandwich. He is hungry but still hasn't taken a bite.

"So, what happened to the other priest, anyway?"

"The Monsignor?"

"No, the younger one. The guy I'd sometimes see at the coffee shop."

"I don't know. We just assume he was taken with everyone else."

"Weren't you there?"

"I was, but I don't know what happened. My memory fails me. I ran outside when the tornado was coming, although I don't remember why, and then everything went black."

He puts a few chips in his mouth, but he can hardly keep them down.

"It all went black," he says again.

Milliken finishes his second sandwich. Chief watches each bite from the corner. He was going to approach him about the car wreck after the service, but he decides to get to the bottom of the pasta salad first. Milliken knows he is there, and he knows he is being watched. He stands next to the father, the mother, and the son. The boy keeps looking at him, but he pretends not to notice.

"You're the guy from the bar, aren't you?"

Milliken ignores the boy's question and stabs the last noodles drenched in Italian dressing.

"Remember, Dad? He was the guy at the bar with the tree."

The dad shrugs. He remembers something about what happened in the creek bed but nothing about the bar. He barely remembers the tree, much less one of the drunks.

"What's your name?" the boy asks.

"Milliken," he says.

The dad's eyes focus on the conversation. He knows what Milliken probably did to his son, and he doesn't have patience for anyone who could even possibly do something like that.

"I saw you at the bar," the boy says. "The day of the tornado. You were sweeping glass."

"I guess I might've been there."

"Do you work there?"

"Not really. More of a patron."

"Did you see the tree fall through the glass?"

"Honestly, kid. I don't remember."

"I was really lucky."

"Why is that?"

"Well, I forgot to pen the cattle, and one got out. I was looking for it when the tornado hit."

"Forgive the question, Kid. But why were you looking for cows in the middle of a tornado?"

The boy's dad puts his hand on the back of his son's neck and then shoots Milliken a look that makes him take a step backward. The dad can smell the alcohol on the man's breath, but he decides not to say anything. He then leads his boy to the table for seconds. Chief throws his paper plate into the five-gallon trash bag hanging from a cafeteria table. He enjoyed his pasta salad and ice water, but that's not why he's here.

The boy's mother starts chatting with Father Nguyen and Professor Anderson. She thanks the priest for the service and tells him she thanks God every day that he survived. She also tells him she attends the early masses because when she was a child there weren't services in the afternoon. Professor Anderson excuses himself and says he'll be right back, although he knows he won't, and he moves back to the table for a final funeral sandwich.

"Did I ever tell you that I almost became a nun, Father?"

"I don't believe you did."

"It's true. I was much younger, though. I wanted to join the order because religion always came naturally to me. It was something I felt was right, and so I went to the convent. It was cheaper than going to other schools, and I enjoyed the routine, but I also got a reputation as a bad girl."

"A bad girl?"

"Yes, Father."

Father Nguyen had been to several convents and never knew any of the women, young or old, to be bad girls.

"You see, I would get bored at night and sneak out with the other girls. In fact, one night I even got them to follow me to a jazz bar. We disappeared into the night with our habits and head covers. Most of the boys were nervous about talking to girls from the convent, but we eventually bumped into a group of them about our age. One of my friends—I believe she is married now—got them to buy us cigarettes. I remember smoking one and watching a man playing the saxophone. His fingers moved quickly, and his head followed the beat.

"Then the waiter approached us and smiled. Most of the girls were from small towns and had never seen a black man. They didn't know what to say, maybe because he was good looking, but I ordered a gin and tonic. He asked if I was old enough to drink, and I told him I forgot my ID. He asked if I swore to God, and I told him I did, and he said he'd bring one. The other girls got ginger ales, and some of them split cigarettes. One of the singers dedicated a song to us, one I had never heard before, but everyone seemed to like it. Before we left, the waiter asked if I'd be back, and I told him I would, God willing, that is. We never came back because we got into so much trouble for sneaking out. Sister Madeleine knew I was the one who led the others astray, and I had to do dishes for a month."

"Is that why you left the order?" Father Nguyen asks.

"Of course not. I loved being there. I just also liked to go out at that age."

"So why did you leave?"

"I wanted to have kids."

"You didn't want to get married?"

"Well, I kind of had to."

Professor Williams enjoys cheese sandwiches, even though the cultures upset her stomach. She puts three slices between bread that is drenched with mayonnaise.

"I had the chance to speak with your student the other day," Professor Williams says.

Professor McKendrick chews his sandwich and asks her to wait by lowering his chin and lifting his index finger. He loves lunch meat because it reminds him of grade school. His mom would always make him a ham sandwich with a single piece of yellow cheese. He thinks about the brown lunch bags waiting for him on the counter and the notes his mother would leave inside.

"Why were you talking to Max, Linda?"

"I bumped into him during the tornado. I was looking for you because we had plans to meet."

"Yeah, I was already at home," he says.

"We had arranged a time, so I figured . . . "

"I knew a tornado was coming. It didn't seem like the moment to be out on the town."

Professor Williams curls her toes and releases a deep breath through her nose.

"Anyway, I found myself in the science building trying to take cover. The tornado came around for a second time, and Max led me to the shelter."

"Just the two of you?"

"Yeah."

"How long were you down there?"

"Honestly, I have no idea. It seemed like an hour, but it might have been longer."

"What did you talk about?"

"He just talked about his research."

"Did you understand any of it?"

Professor Williams frowns.

"I mean, it's complicated stuff, and he doesn't always explain himself well."

Professor Williams releases another long breath through her nose.

"He also hasn't been himself lately. I've worked with a lot of students on serious research projects, ones that could easily be expanded into a dissertation or a professional article, and it's not uncommon for them to get overwhelmed or even become a bit unhinged."

"What do you mean?"

"I'm sure you remember working on your own dissertation, Linda. A research project, especially the writing part, is maddening. It's lonely and exhausting, and you are constantly looking for people who like your idea. When you're young and inexperienced, you can start having strange thoughts. You can think you're right, even when you aren't, and your imagination can run outside the calculations. You can also get desperate, and in that desperation, students make bad decisions."

"What do you mean?"

"Everyone acts irrationally under pressure, especially when working on these types of projects."

"What did he do?"

"I'd really prefer not to talk about it."

"Dammit David, what are you talking about? You can't lead me on like this all the..."

"This stays between you and me."

"Who am I going to tell?"

"He stole something from me. Something that I should have destroyed years ago."

"What do you mean?"

"A long time ago I worked out a theorem for describing something big. Unfortunately, it was too big, the type of project that could consume my entire career. I was on tenure track, and I had to publish a lot quickly, so I decided to put my attention into other things. However, I held on to the pieces, and Max got his hands on them. I gave him a key to my office so he could use my books, but I didn't realize he was looking through my files."

"So, what is it all about?"

"It's a theory of time. It sounds absurd, but there's a way you can bend it, assuming several variables align."

"What do you mean, *bend it*?"

"Well, you can move it backward, kind of like a rewind button. In fact, if you do it right, you can even control it."

Professor Williams smiles. It was like he was telling a joke, and she already knew the punch line.

"And you're the first person to figure all of this out?"

"I'm not sure. Part of me thinks other people know about it. In fact, a guy who used to visit Sunny Side, an old farmer, once sent me a hunk of metal with a piece of paper inside. He discovered it in his backyard and thought it was from a space ship, but it wasn't. I think it was a time capsule, like it came from the future. The language was alien, but it aligns with what I discovered about time, and it even fills a few gaps in my theorem. I became obsessed with it, and it drove me mad. I decided to put it away until I could regain control, but it still hasn't happened. You know there's just something strange about this place, Linda. I'm sure you've heard the rumors. Energy fields. Alien landing zones. Fodder for cults. Sometimes I wonder if someone is behind it all. I wonder if someone from the future is controlling everything we think is the present."

"So, you never built a time machine?"

"This isn't the movies. Reality, especially time, isn't stable. In fact, that's another reason I didn't pursue the project. It's something that is theoretically possible but morally wrong."

"What do you mean?"

"Bending time is like building Frankenstein's monster. The desired outcome may have unforeseen consequences."

"What do you mean?"

"There are these things. I call them ripples. I couldn't figure out how to, well, smooth them out."

"What's a ripple?"

"It's when the past returns to the present. That is, whatever was bent returns in the present, or the future, however you want to understand it. Think of pulling on a guitar string and then releasing it. I figured out how to bend time, you might say, but I never learned how to break it."

"So, everyone would suddenly remember what had happened?"

"Maybe, but I'm not sure. It might just erase everyone's memory. Or something a lot worse. It could be like those movies where someone steps on a bug, and it radically changes the future of our civilization. Anyway, I don't know why you're concerned about this. The whole thing is just a theory, just scratches of ink on an old notebook on my desk."

Professor Williams loses her smile and her appetite. She puts down her plate and looks at the remaining food on the table. The lunch meat is completely gone, but there are still a few pieces of cheese. Her stomach turns, but it isn't from the cultures.

Outside, an old man spits tobacco a few inches from another man's black shoes. The bench is across the street from the service, and the younger man beside him looks lost, like his mind is somewhere else. The old man doesn't know the other guy, but he figures he works at the church. He's wearing black clothes that are dirty and torn, and he hasn't shaved or showered for days. The two don't talk; they just watch the sky and think about the clouds. The old man sees a space ship. The other guy sees a church.

"It's going to rain," the old man says.

The other asks why he thinks that.

"It's that cloud. The one right there, do you see it?"

"I'm afraid I don't. There's a lot of clouds at the end of your finger."

"It looks like a space ship or a bell on a cow. Soon it'll get puffy, and it'll keep getting bigger and darker."

"Is it another tornado?"

"Nah. Just a thunderstorm. The bell will become an anvil, and then it'll poof at the head."

The other man can't find the bell but thinks the space ship

might be the steeple.

"What happened to you, anyway? It looks like you woke up in a dumpster."

"I've just been walking for a few days, that's all."

"With that crutch and limp? I can't imagine you got far."

"That wasn't the point."

"Yeah, I hear you," the old man says, spitting more tobacco on the ground. "Maybe that's what I need. I haven't had a clear thought in years."

"Why is that?"

"I got a couple theories, but it might be something else. It might just be my age. Things don't work like they used to when you get old."

The other man thinks about his future. He doesn't want to die in an empty house with four plates. Then he looks at the church. They probably have his photo at the altar. He can't walk forever, though. He needs a destination. Mexico would be nice. Anywhere is better than here, he reasons.

"I can hear you thinking," the old man says.

The other isn't listening. He's staring at the door. He wonders what photo they used, who cried when they said his name, and if anyone found the other bodies.

"You know you remind me of my boy. He's stubborn, kind of like his old man. Things have been tough around here. Farms are changing hands, and the kids aren't keeping the values. Anyway, he's tried to keep things together, and I admire him for it. He's had a hard time, kind of like me, but for him it's different. I don't know what he's thinking half the time, and I'm not sure his boy does either. My grandson is a good kid, and I think he's more like me than his daddy. He won't be here for long, though. He'll go to school and disappear like everyone else.

"It's like I woke up one day and everyone started to believe in different things, you know? Now there's different gods and different dimensions. It's like someone erased my memory and replaced it with something new. I talk to other people, but they don't get it. They're not like me. They don't know how to read the clouds or predict the seasons. The drought is going to end this year, but no one believes me. They think I'm crazy, but I might be the only one who knows what's going on."

The younger man feels a raindrop and then gets to his feet. He says he'll see the old man around, although he knows he won't. He's got a lot of walking to do, and he'd better get moving.

* * *

Father Nguyen looks at the leftover food, and he thinks about the parable of the fish and the loaves. In it, a large crowd follows Jesus because they have seen him heal the sick and the dying. There is not enough food for the masses, but they come across a boy with two small barley loaves and fish. Jesus blesses the food and then distributes it to his followers. When everyone is full, they fill twelve baskets with leftover barley bread.

Father Nguyen always wondered why the story never specified how the food was multiplied. Did Jesus fill a conjoining field with bread and fish? Did he have a cover over the basket, and the food just appeared when the disciples reached inside? The story creates a logical impossibility: Jesus fed the masses with only two small barley loaves and a couple of small fish. Father Nguyen isn't dumb though. He knows that's the point of the story. Jesus does the impossible. If you follow Him, you will never be hungry.

The volunteers start bagging the leftovers for the homeless shelter. Father Nguyen wishes there was more lunch meat, but the attendees mostly left the cheese and bread. He wishes he could feed the entire shelter with what remained, but he knows he can't. He isn't Jesus, and he doesn't want to be.

Father Nguyen takes a piece of bread and walks outside. He has a bite, and it reminds him of the monastery. That's when he started eating sandwiches for lunch. He looks across the street and sees an old man at a park bench chewing tobacco. He sits down next to the man, and they begin to talk.

"So where are you from, anyway?"

"Vietnam."

"What part?"

"How well do you know Vietnam?"

The old man shrugs.

"Have you been back?"

"Not for a long time. My parents died years ago, and I think my family has forgotten me."

"Your English is good. Did you study it as a boy?"

"I did, and thank you, but not everyone thinks so. I've heard people say things after mass. They laugh at my intonations. It's hard to get it right when speaking to a church full of natives."

"That's their problem."

Father Nguyen smiles.

"I've never been very religious, but I'd never rule out there being a God."

"So why don't you commit to it?"

The old man spits on the ground and then looks to the clouds.

"Because there's too much else out there."

Soon the two hear a voice, but they don't know where it came from. Then there's a silence. They think it must have been the wind, but then they hear it again. The two scan the space around them, but they don't see anyone. Father Nguyen's mind begins to wander, and he closes his eyes. He thinks his time has arrived. His mission will be explained.

The voice comes from above, but it's not God. It's Milliken, and he's hiding in a tree beside them. He also looks drunk. He asks the men if he can sit with them, and Father Nguyen recalls the story of Zaccheus. Father Nguyen offers the man his seat on the bench, but Milliken says that he prefers the ground. He says he likes the dirt because it reminds him of his son.

"He used to spend the entire day looking for worms," he says.

"Is he all grown up now?" Father Nguyen asks.

The man pauses and looks down the empty street. Then he looks up at the clouds. One of them looks like a worm.

"Something like that."

"Well, kids have to grow up and move away. Whether they end up doing one thing or the other doesn't matter. What matters most is that they're happy."

"I suppose so."

He looks back down the road and sees a small figure. He removes a flask from his back pocket, takes a sip, and looks back at the street. He can't tell what it is, but it looks like it's getting closer.

The old man asks for a drink, and he hands him the flask. He recognizes Milliken from somewhere, but he can't remember where. He offers a chew in return, but the other guy turns it down. He says he never liked the taste. The old man shrugs and puts the tin back in his breast pocket.

"You ever think about aliens, Father?" the old man asks.

"Not really."

"You spend all your time thinking about God, and you never wondered if we're the only ones out there?"

"I suppose it's possible."

"Well, what if we ever came into contact, and maybe they don't like us much? You know, the end of the world and all that?"

"I think a lot more people would come to church," the priest says. "Talk of the apocalypse usually brings people to the Lord. The problem is that they only go a couple of times, then they go back to their old ways."

"So you think it's possible, Father?"

"I think if it brings you happiness and not fear, then there is no reason not to believe," he says.

The other man disagrees. He says there isn't anything else out there. He says what's in front of us is what's in front of us, and nothing is going to change that. He slurs his words and constantly looks behind his back to see if Chief is looking for him. Then he looks back down the street, and he makes out the figure again. It is low to the ground and is moving closer. He takes another sip and watches it, but he can't tell what it is.

"If it was up to me we'd all be left alone. No aliens. No gods.

No books. No crazy religions. They all keep us from seeing what's in front of us. They make us blind, and they make us dumb."

The other two don't know what to say.

"Let me try that," Father Nguyen asks.

The man hands him the flask, and he takes a long drink. He keeps it down, but he starts to cough.

"That's not the easiest stuff to lean on," the old man tells him.

Father Nguyen looks at the darkening cloud shaped liked an anvil.

"You know it's strange that I wound up in this town and not any of the others," the priest says. "I sometimes think it was part of a bigger plan. My great grandfather or my great-great grandfather, I can never remember which, came here to work. He arrived with people from all over Asia, but most just called them Chinese— well, that and other names. Anyway, he got a job working for the railroad. His goal was to make enough money to return home, but he never did. You couldn't just fly back in those days. You had to take a train to the coast and then a ship across the Pacific. It was long, expensive, and very dangerous."

He reaches out his hand, and the man on the ground hands him the flask.

"Anyway, he worked with other immigrants, and part of their job was to build the railroad. He wrote letters to his family every month, but he never knew if they arrived. The wages were bad, and sometimes they didn't pay the workers anything. The work was dangerous too. There were falling rocks, long hours, dirty houses, and unclean drinking water. He got into a fight with another worker over rations and almost got stabbed. He wrote about it in a letter that he sent his wife, which is now in my living room, along with the others. The last one his wife received said he was going to leave his job. He said they wanted him to start using dynamite, and he knew he'd be killed. He also said he'd write one more letter, a love letter, but that he'd deliver it himself.

"He never came home, though. The facts are unclear, but it seems like he died a few days or weeks later. We never found his last letter, but I have faith that it still exists. If I keep praying, I know that I'll find it."

The old man swallows his tobacco, and then starts hacking.

"Where was your grandad working?" he asks.

"I'm not certain. A lot of the towns didn't have names, but it was likely somewhere in the Midwest, probably in a town like this one."

"And how did you get to Hooper, exactly, Father?"

"I was sent here by the Lord."

The drunk man on the ground identifies the figure in the distance. It's a young boy moving on his hands and knees. It looks like he's on the pavement, but he isn't certain. He takes another drink to focus his eyes, and he sees his boy removing earthworms from the pavement. It's not the first time he's seen the figure, and he's sure he'll see it again.

He thinks about how the past affects the present. Then he thinks about how the present affects the past.

Maybe he washed away in the river.

Maybe I did do it.

My memory still fails me.

Maybe I can go back in time.

The old man pulls out his tobacco, spits, and rubs the juices into the pavement with his boot. The priest and the old man say goodbye. The man on the ground doesn't know where they are going, but he figures they have somewhere to be. He looks back down the road, but the boy is gone.

Then he sees two new figures. One is Chief, and the other is someone he doesn't recognize. Another raindrop falls, and then it starts to sprinkle. Soon it will be raining hard, and the earthworms will surface from their holes and wash onto the sidewalks. The birds will begin to eat the worms, and fishermen will pick them from the ground and put them into containers. The storm might get stronger and may produce a tornado. The sirens will then sound, and everyone will head for shelter. Some will believe this truly is the end, and others will think nothing of it.

It's spring in the Midwest.

Nothing to see here.
Just another round of April warnings.

Chief tells Milliken to take it easy. He says they'll handle the drunk driving case, but now isn't the time. He tells him he has something else to do. He also says he can relax about his son. He says he found something that might prove he's innocent.

Milliken isn't sure if he's dreaming. He has already convinced himself that he had done it. Maybe he didn't, or maybe the evidence and everyone else was wrong.

Chief walks past the park bench and approaches a black town car that is parked down the street. He asks the driver to roll down his window and then tells him that they need to talk.

* * *

The mayor replays the day in his mind. He does so every few hours, especially in the late afternoon, and anytime he's alone. The plan was simple, and they had done it before, but this time something went wrong. Everything would have worked out cleanly. Chief would have been just another picture at the front of the church, and nobody would have asked a question. Instead, The Russian is dead, and the sheriff isn't. What's strange is that he hasn't heard from law enforcement since it happened. Chief hasn't filed a report, and the news hasn't said a word about the event. Around town, people said Nana and The Russian exchanged words at the bar, and Chief got caught in the cross fire. The mayor wonders what Chief is planning. He figures there's no reason to worry. He still knows people more powerful than a local sheriff.

He goes outside and observes the clouds. He sees one that looks like a goat and another that looks like a tree. Soon the town car pulls up, and The mayor gets inside. He shuffles in his chair until he's comfortable in his seat, and the window between him and the driver soon rolls down.

"Take me back to the office," the mayor says.

The driver is wearing his hat, but he looks different. He has large features, a grey ponytail, and a grin extending to both his ears. The mayor reaches for the handle, but the door is locked from the inside.

"We're not going to your office," Chief tells him. "We're going to take a little drive out to that land I was telling you about. I think you'll really like it."

Acknowledgements

Perhaps nothing inspired this book more than a poster outside the restroom at the old Hinky Dinky supermarket on 120th and Center in Omaha. It showed an enormous twister ready to swallow a farmhouse in the middle of nowhere, and on the top, right-hand corner were big, white letters that read "Tornado Shelter Below." The image terrified me each time I went to the bathroom there as a child, and it made me wonder every spring if our home in Prairie Lane would meet the same demise as the farmhouse on the wall a few feet from the lobster tank.

Readers of *April Warnings* will find tornados, aliens, and even a cultist or two, but I continue to find my childhood. I can't reread these stories without thinking about my parents, Robert and Roberta, who always let me be me, and my siblings, Mike and Michelle, who always kept me in line. Also important were my other families, people like the Vails, the Cockles, the Putnams, and so many others I'm probably forgetting.

I should also recognize Chief, a natural storyteller who drove our bus from Denver to Winter Park on a 12th-grade field trip when I worked as a high school Spanish teacher. His stories aren't necessarily the ones here, but they inspired the plots behind the titles that bear his name. My gratitude also extends to the baristas who kept the doors open for me at the now-closed Café Europa in Denver. It was there that I found a quiet place to write the closing chapters of *April Warnings*. Other thanks go to Brian at Innisfree Poetry Bookstore & Café in Boulder and BookBar in Denver. Their support of local writers is extraordinary. My appreciation also goes out to David Harper, Scott Spanbauer, David Wolf, Michael

Adam Carroll, Andrés Prieto, María José Maddox, Will Cockle, and Spencer Putnam for reading iterations of the stories or the full manuscript. I must also recognize the many teachers who I have had throughout my life at places like Westside High School, Simpson College, and the University of Colorado, Boulder who have encouraged me in my writing.

I'd also like to recognize the bus drivers at the Regional Transportation District in Denver who brave two dangerous stretches of highways on a daily basis (Interstate 25 and Highway 36). Without their important labor, I would not be able to write for a few precious hours every day during my commute, and I subsequently never would have finished my manuscript. And, of course, my unending thanks to Minerva Laveaga Luna and her team at Veliz Books for taking a chance on a batch of stories about the North American Midwest.

Lastly, and perhaps most importantly, this book would not have been possible without the love of my life, Erin, whose support provides me each day with the motivation I need to always keep writing.

About the Author

Mark Pleiss is a writer in Denver. He publishes fiction, book reviews, scholarly criticism, and essays, and his work has appeared in *Tupelo Quarterly*, *Colorado Review*, *The Omaha Pulp*, *Sequel*, *Fine Lines*, *Palimpsest*, *The Chronicle of Higher Education*, *The Denver Post*, and elsewhere. He worked as a freelance journalist for *The Omaha World-Herald* and *The Des Moines Register* before completing a doctorate in Spanish Literature and teaching at St. Olaf College, CU Boulder, and Metro State University Denver. He is from Omaha, Nebraska.